THE SILENT HOUSE

H. M. LYNN

Boldwood

First published in Great Britain in 2025 by Boldwood Books Ltd.

Cover Design by Lisa Horton

Cover Images: Callum Ollason / Arcangel and Shutterstock

A CIP catalogue record for this book is available from the British Library.

Paperback ISBN 978-1-83603-811-5

Large Print ISBN 978-1-83603-812-2

Hardback ISBN 978-1-83603-810-8

Ebook ISBN 978-1-83603-813-9

Kindle ISBN 978-1-83603-814-6

Audio CD ISBN 978-1-83603-805-4

MP3 CD ISBN 978-1-83603-806-1

Digital audio download ISBN 978-1-83603-809-2

This book is printed on certified sustainable paper. Boldwood Books is dedicated to putting sustainability at the heart of our business. For more information please visit https://www.boldwoodbooks.com/about-us/sustainability/

Boldwood Books Ltd, 23 Bowerdean Street, London, SW6 3TN

www.boldwoodbooks.com

ALSO BY H. M. LYNN

The Holly Berry Sweet Shop Series

The Sweet Shop of Second Chances

Love Blooms at the Second Chances Sweet Shop

High Hopes at the Second Chances Sweet Shop

Family Ties at the Second Chances Sweet Shop

Sunny Days at the Second Chances Sweet Shop

A Summer Wedding at the Second Chances Sweet Shop

Snowflakes Over the Second Chances Sweet Shop

Happy Ever After at the Second Chances Sweet Shop

The Wildflower Lock Series

New Beginnings at Wildflower Lock

Coffee and Cake at Wildflower Lock

Blue Skies Over Wildflower Lock

Forever Love at Wildflower Lock

Standalone Novels

In at the Deep End

The Side Hustle

Hannah Lynn writing as H. M. Lynn

The Head Teacher

The Student

The Valentine's Date

The Silent House

To the Books and Biscuits writing group.

1

'Imogen, I know I've already taken up a lot of your time with questions today, but I wondered if you might have time for just a couple more?'

No, I want to say. *No, I don't. This whole thing is tedious and dry and I hate it. The only reason you've had any of my time is because my agent, Orla, insisted and she's a good friend and the reason I make so much money. If I had my way, I'd never speak to any of you. Ever. Speaking to you distracts from my painting, my art, my life. So no, I don't have time for a couple more questions.* That's what I want to say, and it's not just because I hate talking to journalists or critics or whatever this one claims to be. Today is manic. Today, Patrick and I are packing up our belongings and moving to the middle of nowhere, and I don't use that expression lightly.

The house is called Cedar Wood Cottage, but the small cluster of houses it's part of is so insignificant it isn't even considered a village. No bus stop. No quaint little green. No old phone box converted into a book exchange the way so many have been recently. Our address mentions the road name and the nearest town, which is four miles away. That's how in the middle of nowhere we are.

If that won't give me the inspiration to create some incredible paintings, I don't know what will.

'Imogen? Would that be okay? Do you have a couple of minutes to keep talking?'

The voice at the end of the phone brings me back to the moment.

'Yes,' I say in reflex, though it was absolutely not the answer I wanted to give.

'Fantastic,' she continues. 'Now, Imogen, I'm sure you won't mind me saying, but you're known for being an incredibly private person.'

'I'm sure I'm not *that* private,' I say sharply. 'I wouldn't be doing this interview if I was.'

She lets out a strained laugh. 'Well, let's be honest, so far we've only talked about your past exhibition and your upcoming work and your exciting change in style.'

'Sorry, but I assumed that was what your readers would want to know about. Being that you're an *art* publication.'

I don't mean to be so snappy. It's not what I'm like in real life at all, but these things set me on edge. I can already tell she's going to start digging, and I want to stop. I want to hang up the phone, but then I'd come across as moody and unhelpful. And I'm not.

She's just a journalist. Prying.

'Oh, absolutely. The readers thoroughly enjoy hearing about your exhibitions and your process, but they would also love to know more about the inspiration behind your artwork. What drives you to keep producing at such a prolific level? What's caused this shift away from the introspective darkness of all your previous work to something far more uplifting and mainstream? From what I've seen, the famous Cromford Blue barely features any more. Is there a personal reason you shifted away from those tones? I'm aware that the poverty in which you grew up impacted your work significantly, and your mother's untimely death, which, according to our sources – '

'I'm done,' I say, cutting her off before she can continue.

'Sorry?'

'I know you want to turn this into some sensationalist piece of writing with a clickbait headline to get people reading it, but that's not what I agreed to. You wanted an interview about my art, and you've got it.'

'That's not what I was after at all, I was just – '

'This has overrun now by quite a bit. If you've got any other questions about my art, please contact my agent. Oh, and remember, you need approval before you go to print with that.'

I hang up before letting out a sigh that transforms into a groan before it's done. Orla is going to be pissed at me. I know she is. She'll give me a long lecture about how the marketing is just as important as the art and how there's a good chance that magazine won't want to work with me again, but we both know that's not true. One thing about being *notoriously private* – the journalist's words, not mine – is that they'll grapple for every piece of me they can get. And I don't give it to them.

'Everything all right?' Patrick says from the driver's seat. 'It sounded like things were getting a bit prickly there.'

As I turn to look at him, tension flickers along my jawline. 'Just because I'm pissed off at some random journalist,' I say, 'doesn't mean I'm not still pissed off at you, too.'

He drops his chin slightly and bites down on his bottom lip. It's an expression that makes him look so much younger. Patrick is in his late forties and sixteen years my senior, though he very rarely acts it. Normally, it's moments like this when his youthful side creeps out – even if it is a guilty pout – that I soften towards him.

But I'm struggling today. I'm just too mad at him.

As I turn back and stare out of the window, I try to make myself see reason. Maybe I should have expected it. If you marry a man sixteen years older than you with an already grown-up child, there are bound to be bumps in the road, especially if said child is as difficult as Prim. She'd already pegged me as the evil stepmother-slash-gold-digger before she'd even met me, and though I've tried my hardest to show her that's not who I am, progress has been slow going. Moving away from London was meant to be a fresh start for us. A chance for us to get out of the shadows of his ex-wife and the hold his daughter has on him, but I can see that it's never going to happen. Not now he's gone and done this.

2

Patrick takes his hand off the gearstick and rests it on my knee. I know he wants me to turn and look at him, but I can't. I'm doing everything I can to stay calm about the situation. To act like it's no big deal – but it is. Not to him, I get that, but to me it's changed things. Not between Patrick and me, but about our new home together.

'Imogen, I never would've done this if I'd known how much it was going to upset you,' he says. His eyes continually glance from the road to me, hoping I'll make eye contact with him. 'You know I wouldn't have done that. I'd never do anything to upset you. Not ever. But especially not now, not with everything going on. I thought I was doing something kind. Building bridges. You get that, don't you?'

I don't want to reply. I want to stay mad at him, but today isn't the day for me to be angry with my husband, and not just because we are moving into our forever home. Ten days ago, I had two viable embryos implanted in my uterus. Two balls of cells with the potential of growing into so much more. The potential of becoming mine and Patrick's children. In less than a week, I'll be able to do a pregnancy test and see whether they have implanted, but until then, all I can do is hope. Hope and stay positive. Unfortunately, the news that Patrick has given Prim a spare key to my new home is making that hard to do.

My heel bounces up and down just above the footwell. A sign of frustration, or just pent-up energy? Both probably. I should've anticipated this before the removal men came and collected all our boxes. My bike is in the back of their lorry, so I couldn't have used that, but I should've gone for a run. I get fidgety if I don't move enough, and I can feel the antsy twitchiness creeping in. Not that I don't have a reason to feel antsy. Knowing that Prim has a way into our house, regardless of whether I want her there, is more than enough to make me feel nervous.

Finally, I let out an exasperated sigh. 'I don't know why you didn't ask me about it first,' I say. 'Why didn't you at least check I was okay with it?'

'You're right. I didn't think...' Patrick takes his eyes off the road to look at me. 'It was just – she was so upset about us moving out here. About being so far away.'

'We are two hours from London, Patrick. There's a train station a twenty-minute drive away that goes direct.'

'I know that, I do, but she's twenty-one. She's practically a kid. And you know she still struggles with... well, the affair.'

My jaw clenches again. Twenty-one and still a kid? Really? I was half her age when I had to deal with some pretty screwed-up shit, and I'm not saying I'd wish that upon anyone, but at what point is he expecting her to take responsibility for anything?

In one way Patrick's right, though. The affair he and I had while he was still with Prim's mother, Arabella, is the reason Prim hates me so much. I shattered her illusion of having a perfect family. And it *was* an illusion. Patrick's told me more than enough to know that.

Still, the affair was the reason Prim tipped red wine down my wedding dress when she turned up two hours into the reception, already drunk out of her mind. It's also the reason I had to have security at my last exhibition opening – because the time before, she turned up drunk, with a tin of red emulsion paint, which she tried to throw over one of my pieces of art. Prim's the reason I've wanted to get out of London. Because even one of the busiest cities in the world feels claustrophobic when you've got Patrick's daughter, not to mention his ex, living there. That's the bit that Prim can't seem to get her head around. Yes, Patrick and I had an affair, but we didn't do it to cause people pain and it wasn't like it was me that did the pursuing. Patrick had been trapped with Arabella in a mentally abusive relationship for years, and I offered him the freedom he craved. No, that's not right. I offered him the freedom he *deserved*.

The attraction was immediate for both of us, but we didn't act on it straight away. Even when his visits to the gallery became so regular that Orla started commenting on how perhaps he was after more than just art, it took a couple of months before either of us was brave enough to make a move. Patrick wasn't someone who played around or cheated, despite the vile things Arabella did to him. And yes, that included having affairs. Then there was the age gap issue. Sixteen years isn't enormous, but I was, and always will be, closer to Prim's age than his. I think he was fearful that one day I would turn around and decide it had just been a bit of fun and leave him to pick up the pieces of his life that I had broken apart.

Besides, freeing himself from Arabella's grasp wasn't easy. She controlled so many aspects of his life. She told him what clothes to wear, who to go out for dinner with. When he started his law practice, she even picked out the office furniture he was allowed to have. Arabella wouldn't let him breathe – that's what he said I did for him. I allowed him to breathe again.

One day when he turned up at the art gallery, I took the plunge and asked him if perhaps he would like to come to my studio to see some pieces of art I was working on. He accepted the offer and the rest, as they say, is history.

'Why the hell have you not already found someone?' he said to me one Monday morning as we lay in my apartment. The rain hammered on the roof as our bodies were wrapped up in the white sheets and one another. 'You are the most incredible woman I've ever met.'

'It's complicated,' I said. 'I guess expecting someone to be with me through thick and thin has always felt a bit far-fetched.'

'I'm not here because I think it's going to be easy,' he'd replied. 'I wouldn't be planning on leaving my wife if all I wanted was easy. You can tell me; you can tell me everything. I want you to.'

And so I did. That day was the first day I'd ever spoken to a partner about what happened with my mother. The first time I'd spoken to anyone about it properly. Other than shrinks, of course.

In those twenty minutes, I must have shown him a thousand red flags, and I half expected him to leave and never contact me again, but he didn't. Instead, he listened to what I said and tears welled in his eyes. Tears for me. For the child I had been and what I had gone through. When I was done, he pulled me into him and kissed me gently on the forehead.

'My darling, I am so sorry you ever had to go through that. No child should ever have to suffer what you went through.' I stayed silent, wiping the tears from my cheeks. Tears I didn't want to show him, and yet he placed his fingers beneath my chin and tilted it up so that I looked straight into his eyes. 'Whatever you want, I will make it happen. I promise you that. Imogen, you are my future. I want to grow old with you. Have children with you – if that's what you want. I want us to have it all. I want you to have it all.'

Before that moment I had never understood when people said their heart could burst because it was so full, but I did then. That day, my heart swelled to such a size I thought it might break free from my chest. 'I want that too,' I said. 'It's all I want. You are all I want.'

The next day, he saw a divorce lawyer.

I thought Arabella would kick up more of a fuss and make it difficult for him to leave. At the very least, I assumed she would turn Prim against him. But all she wanted was his money. And money is something both Patrick and I knew we could earn more of.

Now, here we are, two years later, driving down the winding roads that will lead to our forever home. And when I think of that memory, and how I never felt truly seen before Patrick, it's hard to stay mad at him. I might just have to change the locks at some point, that's all.

3

I grew up in London. Not in a large, light, breezy terrace house like Patrick had, before he handed it over to Arabella as part of the divorce package, or even a compact but clean flat in a nice area of the city, like I was renting before we got together. The flats I grew up in were the type they show on crime documentaries late at night, with grey tower blocks, broken windows, and gangs of youths sitting outside, smoking cigarettes as they take apart a burned-out car. I grew up in the type of place where I'd go to bed at night listening to the man in the flat above beat his wife so hard that he dislocated her jaw. Where I had drug addicts getting confused about where they lived and hammering on my door at two in the morning, while my mother just told me to put my fingers in my ears and wait for it to be over. I don't want my child to grow up in the type of place where she'll have to call the police at eleven o'clock at night because there's a baby screaming in the flat next door, and you know the mother has gone and left them. In fairness, had my mother not been passed out drunk on the sofa then it wouldn't have fallen to a ten-year-old to call the emergency services, but that's hardly the worst position she put me in. Still, I have mixed memories of the city.

I'd often thought about moving somewhere with open fields and the room for a big outside studio, but I didn't think Patrick would move that far away from his family or practice, but after a month of fruitless searching, I'd made the suggestion.

'What about if we cast our search further afield?' I said, trying to sound casual about the whole thing.

'How far afield were you thinking?' he said. 'Surrey? Kent?'

'Maybe somewhere further. I've always loved the Cotswolds.'

He tilted his head to the side, and his bottom lip disappeared as he visibly chewed the idea over.

'It could be doable.'

A flurry of excitement fluttered through me and even now I remember the way I felt, as if I had drifted out of my body and landed in someone else's. Someone who had all the things childhood me had only dreamed about. Not that I don't give myself credit where credit's deserved. I worked hard to get to where I am.

Naturally, there were logistics that came with such a move. Patrick's office is in London and that wasn't going to change, meaning we needed to be somewhere commutable. Thankfully, I'm a fan of logistics and logic and it didn't take long for me to narrow down the search based on distances to the nearest stations. Then it was just a case of waiting to see what the estate agent found.

The waiting was the hardest part. Each day, both our inboxes were flooded with unsuitable properties, until a Tuesday morning six months ago when Patrick rang me from the office.

'I've just been sent one,' he said. 'It's not on the market yet, so the photos aren't the best, but it used to be a farm building. A cottage for the workers or something like that. And it comes with an outbuilding that's already got electricity. The estate agent says it'll be perfect for a studio. I'll send you the photos now.'

Thirty seconds after he hung up the call, my phone began buzzing. The images came through one after another. Like Patrick said, they weren't great, but they were enough.

'Wow,' I said as I showed them straight to Orla. We had met for a coffee just to catch up, although it had turned into a full-scale marketing meeting and I was grateful for the distraction Patrick had provided. Orla doesn't have the ability to shut off from work, and every get-together ends up a business meeting. It's something I both love and hate about her.

'Those views,' she said with a sigh. 'That would be incredible. And no neighbours either. Bliss.'

'I think there are a couple of other houses nearby,' I said, reading the scant text Patrick had provided. 'But you're right. Those are the type of views I could get used to.'

'Not to mention it would be the perfect place to raise a family,' she added.

Orla was the only other person who knew that Patrick and I were trying to get pregnant, although I had planned on using the coffee date to tell her about our decision to start IVF privately. Neither of us are ignorant of how Patrick is going to be an older dad this time around. And sure, IVF might have only changed things by six months to a year, but the older you get, the more those months count. And it's not like we lack the money.

'So, are you going to see it?' Orla asked, still looking at the photo.

A moment later, my phone buzzed again with another message from Patrick.

> Viewing at 11 a.m. tomorrow. We're going to need to leave early.

4

The house was a state. The garden was overgrown and we couldn't even get into the outbuilding, and yet we put in an offer that evening.

'I know it'll take time,' Patrick said, 'but it'll be worth it. I can really see us here.'

'So can I. It's going to be perfect.'

The entire journey back, my cheeks ached, I was grinning so much, and I wasted no time in telling Orla that this was it. We had found the home of our dreams. Or at least the house that would become the home of our dreams, after some serious renovations.

Though we made the decision to buy the place after only a fifteen-minute tour, the process of getting into the house was agonisingly slow. While I don't know the ins and outs of the previous owner's situation, it felt as though they were being forced to sell, rather than choosing to, and more than once I felt certain it was going to fall through.

'Maybe we should give up,' I said to Patrick several times

over the following months. 'We could just pull out of the sale and find somewhere different.'

'We could, but think about how long it took us to find this place. We might have to wait another six months until something else suitable comes up and then we might still have to go through all this again. Is that a chance you want to take? Especially when it could all be completed any day now.'

It was a logical response, and I'm almost always swayed by logic. Besides, the house had so many things we were after. It's in the middle of nowhere, but not entirely isolated. It has far-reaching countryside views, but is only twenty minutes from the station with a direct train to London. And it has the potential to improve and extend the way I have always dreamed about. No, it wasn't perfect in many ways. And yet it was perfect in every way. Which is why we waited.

'You're not gonna be mad at me all day, are you?' Patrick says, dragging me back to the moment. 'I'd hate to think that on the first day in our new home, you're cross with me.'

Once again, his eyes are off the road to look at me and there's genuine worry creasing his forehead. It doesn't matter whether or not I want to be mad at him. Nothing is worse to me than seeing Patrick think he's screwed up. Arabella made him feel like that with almost every decision he made for the last two decades. When I accepted his proposal, I promised myself I would never become that sort of spouse. The type who would punish their other half emotionally when things didn't go their way. Of course, this situation is a little more complicated than that, but I can see that right now, Patrick needs my assurance. He needs to know that I'm not going to flip out on him the way Arabella always used to do.

'You know I can never stay mad at you,' I say. 'And I know you didn't do it to deliberately hurt me.'

'I really didn't,' he says as a wash of relief floods his face.

'Then all is forgiven. But can you please send a message to Prim, telling her she needs to text before she visits? That she can't just turn up whenever she wants?'

'I will do that as soon as we get there.' His relief turns into a smile, which flickers on his lips. 'Which, according to the satnav, is only six minutes away. Are you ready for this?'

'I've been ready for months.'

My stomach is fluttering with butterflies and I find myself thinking that this must be what it's like for a child at Christmas. The anticipation. The excitement. The knowledge that unimaginable delights are waiting for them around the corner. I never had that myself, but I'm going to revel in the feeling now, and I'm going to make sure my child gets to feel it, too.

As Patrick carries on driving, I look out the window at the myriad of colours, trying to spot any familiar landmarks, though it's tricky when it's all trees and fields. One thing is definite, though. Summer is well and truly over. 'It looks different now, don't you think?' Patrick says, echoing my thoughts. 'Yes. I think I might like it even more than before.'

When we first visited, the countryside was bursting with life. Trees were laden with blossoms, while wildflowers crowded the verges. Now, there is very little green in sight. The leaves have shed the trees in droves, displaying the spindly, brittle branches beneath, and the fields are tones of yellow and ochre. Already I can feel a dozen painting ideas whirring in my mind. My work always has an abstract edge to it, but it's rooted in nature, and I know exactly what colour palette my next couple of pieces are going to feature.

'I can't wait to go for a cycle down these lanes,' I say as we get closer and closer to our destination. 'I might go for a ride tomorrow.'

Patrick looks at me, his eyes narrowing. 'Do you really think that's a good idea? The nurses said you were meant to take it easy.'

'I'm pretty sure a slow cycle will be absolutely fine. It's not as if I'm going to be doing velodrome speeds. Besides, my body is used to doing four spinning classes a week. I'd be more worried if I stopped exercising.'

'Maybe,' he says. 'Right, this is it. The lane to the cottages is just up here.'

I don't know why I feel the urge to hold my breath. It's not like I'm expecting any great surprises. I've seen the house twice in person, thousands of times in photos and online. But this is the first time I've seen it since it's been mine. My home.

'There it is,' Patrick says. 'Just up there.'

Our house is at the end of the lane. First, we pass a pair of small semi-detached cottages, one of which has a light on in it. Those two cottages make up the entirety of our neighbours. It's insane, particularly when I think about how there were four other flats on the same floor as mine in my childhood home. The estate agent didn't have much information on the owners of the cottages, apart from how they keep themselves to themselves, but who knows, maybe we'll strike up some sort of friendship over time. If we don't, it's not like we're living on top of each other. There's at least fifty feet between the nearest one and ours.

'Are you all right to open the gate?' Patrick says. 'When we get the tip to empty the junk from the studio, we'll put the gate in it too. Why on earth someone would feel they needed something like this all the way out here is a mystery to me.'

The gate is definitely a strange addition. The five pieces of wood look like they're only being held in place by a few nails and it's completely superfluous given the large gap beside it that anyone could walk straight through. Still, we need it open for the car and removal lorry, yet as I unclip my belt, Patrick's hand lands on mine.

'Maybe I should do it,' he says. 'You know, in case you are pregnant?'

I'm about to laugh at the comment when I realise he's serious. 'Patrick, I can open a gate. Don't worry.'

With a slight chuckle still lingering on my lips, I lean forward and kiss him on the cheek before unclipping my belt and climbing out of the car.

Outside, I shake my head and free the laugh from my lungs. The gate has to weigh less than some of the big canvasses or paint tins I work with, and there's no way I'm going to let him stop me from carrying those. Although I think maybe we're going to have to set some ground rules about what I am and am not going to do if I find out the IVF has worked, otherwise Patrick is going to have me on bedrest from the day that test shows positive.

I'm still imagining how much he's going to want to mollycoddle me when I reach the gate, though as I go to put my hands to the top bar I freeze. There's something hanging on the fence post. Something I couldn't see from the car and even though I'm standing right beside it, for a second I can't make out what it is.

'What the hell?'

As the words leave my mouth, the reality of what I'm staring at hits. My stomach somersaults as a wave of nausea washes over me.

5

Normally my trigger is blood. Either the sight or the smell, if it's strong enough. One deep inhale or glance at a fresh streak of red and my temperature soars. I go from feeling perfectly okay to so hot it's like my skin's going to melt. Beads of sweat pour down my face, but the heat is always temporary. A heartbeat later, I feel as though I'd been plunged into icy water. The sweating continues as my chest tightens, though 'tighten' feels like a casual word for what happens to me. It's like my ribs are being crushed. As though ropes are tied around me and with each inhale, they are pulled with such force it shatters my bones and causes the shards to pierce my lungs.

That's how it used to be, anyway. How it used to start.

While my shattered ribcage stole the air from my lungs, my throat narrowed so that I could barely wheeze, and that was when the dizziness started. Sometimes I'd catch myself before I passed out completely, but not always. Once, in an art class, a fellow student had a nosebleed. As a flash of heat burned through my body, I knew exactly what was to come. I tried to ready myself for it. To lower myself onto the ground away from everyone else, but I didn't have time. It was so sudden. When I passed out, I collapsed onto my easel, which fell onto another student's, wrecking not only my project, but also the one they had been working on for the last month. That's when I knew I had to do more. I had to sever myself from those memories. But that's something easier said than done.

Closing my eyes, I draw a lungful of air in through my nose and begin tapping a spot on my eyebrow.

'This is not the same,' I say as I exhale with a blow. 'You are safe here. You are safe.'

I move the location of my tapping around.

'This is life. Things live and things die. But you are safe. You are safe.'

I focus on the breaths, the tapping, the words. Anything but what I saw. I don't know how long I stand here, but as my fingers tap at my collarbone, I realise I'm still standing. There's no sweat trickling down my spine. No wheezing as I struggle to remain upright. I'm okay.

'Imogen, what is it?' I open my eyes to find Patrick standing beside me. 'What happened? Is it the pregnancy? Are you okay?'

I shake my head before gesturing towards the gatepost. That's when he sees them, too.

'Oh.'

'Why would someone do that?' I say. A pair of dead birds hang from our gate. Their necks are tied with bright orange string, but it's their eyes that haunt me. White opaque spheres gaze out without a hint of life and yet it's like they're looking everywhere and nowhere at once. As if death has given them that ability. 'What kind of sick person does this?'

'I think they're pheasants,' Patrick says.

'I don't care what kind of bird they are. Someone did this deliberately.' I look around me. This is not the type of place that you would drive through accidentally. It was hard enough for us to find, even though we knew where it was. No, this is a threat. I can feel it. 'Please, Patrick, can you move them off there? I just want them gone. Now.'

He nods. 'Of course.'

I'm not the kind of person who thinks men should do all the manual jobs in a home. In fact, I'd rather do things myself, whether that's building a cabinet or changing the oil in my car. At least that way, I know it's done properly. But dead animals? That's something I can't handle. Though, it's not exactly Patrick's forte either. He's a forty-eight-year-old lawyer who's lived his entire life in London. The closest he comes to raw meat is when he orders steak tartare, which he never does when he's with me. I've been a strict vegetarian since I was fourteen and seeing something like this reminds me why.

Patrick grimaces slightly as he reaches out and lifts the birds by the string around their necks. As he moves them, I force myself to take another look. He's right – they *are* pheasants, judging by the colour. A male and a female. But why the hell would someone do this?

'What do you think I should do with them?' Patrick asks. 'Can I just put them in the bin?'

'I don't know… Throw them in the hedge maybe,' I say, but as he moves, I change my mind. 'Actually, we might get rats and things if we just put them in the hedge. Maybe the bin *is* a better idea.'

I move towards the gap by the gate, ready to open the bin for Patrick so he can dump the birds as quickly as possible. But as I step to the side, someone speaks.

'So, I see you've found my gift then. Was worried you weren't going to get here today. I almost took them back.'

6

I draw my eyes away from Patrick and the dead pheasants to the woman walking up the grass verge towards us. She's kitted out appropriately with wellington boots and a thick wax jacket. But the most striking thing about her is the creature at her side – a scruffy, long-haired grey dog that stands near hip height to the old woman. The dog's upper lip twitches as if about to snarl, but she tugs sharply on its lead.

'Brutus, that's enough,' she says, her voice firm. 'We came to give the new neighbours a nice welcome, not scare them. Don't worry, his bark's a lot worse than his bite. Which is more than you can say for some folks, eh?' She lets out a chuckle, and from the way she's looking at me, it's clear she expects me to laugh too, but I can't. There are too many things to process right now.

'I'm sorry,' I say, trying to focus. 'Did you just say this was a *gift*? These dead birds—'

'The brace,' she interrupts.

'The what?'

'The brace. That's what we call it. A cock and a hen make a brace. Little housewarming gift, you know. My nephew, he shoots pheasants, and, well, I've had him dropping them by the last few days. The estate agent said you were moving in soon, so I wanted to have a little something ready for you. Glad you've come now, though. I've been having pheasant for tea all week, and to be honest, I'm getting fed up with it. Not to mention I was a bit worried about maggots with that one.'

'Maggots?' Patrick asks, holding the brace further away from his body.

'Oh, they're just in the feathers. And only because it's been hanging for a few days there. Doesn't affect the meat. But I'd get them plucked soon if I were you.'

I'm pretty sure my jaw is hanging loose, but I can't close my mouth. This woman is insane. She has to be. I'm certain she's telling the truth – she really put a pair of dead birds on our gate as a welcome gift. But who does something like that? Apparently, country folk.

'Well, that's very kind of you,' I manage, 'but actually, I'm a vegetarian.'

'Vegetarian?' She looks at me like I've just slapped her. 'What'd you do that for?'

'It's just been a long time... I don't really believe—' I cut myself off. I can already tell this topic of conversation won't end well. 'Patrick eats meat, though. But I'm not sure he knows how to pluck them.' I raise my eyebrows at him. 'Do you?'

'Umm, I could give it a go?'

With a loud sigh, the woman marches over and snatches the pheasants from Patrick. 'Guess it's over to me again, then. Stew all right with you?' she asks.

'Pheasant stew?'

'I've got a few good potatoes from the garden and a couple of herbs. I was gonna roast it tonight if you hadn't shown up, but stew's probably best. Then you can take some home.'

'We wouldn't want to impose,' Patrick says, and from his tone, I can tell he's telling the woman that we have no desire whatsoever to go to hers for pheasant stew, but either she doesn't hear that, or she just doesn't care.

'Right, well, I assume you've got the removal men coming now?'

'Yes,' I say, eager to escape the situation. 'Any minute now, actually. We need to get inside and figure out where they're putting everything.'

'Well, you need time to sort yourselves out. Get cleaned up. Shall we say seven?'

'Seven?'

'For the pheasant stew. For him, not you, obviously. I'll do a jacket potato for you. I'm the cottage on the left,' she says, gesturing down the lane. 'The one with the blue door. So, does seven work?'

'I... I...' I don't want to spend our first night in our new home at this bizarre woman's house, especially not with that dog eyeing me like a chew toy. I rack my brain for an excuse, but before I can she's speaking again.

'You're not going to turn down your first invitation, are you?' she says in a way that makes my skin prickle slightly, though it's Patrick she's looking at as she speaks. I'm sure he's about to explain to her, a little more firmly perhaps, that heading out on our first night is not something we plan on doing. Finally, he speaks up.

'Seven sounds good,' he says.

I feel my jaw drop, but I can't say anything. The woman's mouth curls and it's the closest thing to a smile I've seen on her so far.

'Good. No need to bring any drink – I've got plenty. You do drink, don't you?' She throws me a knowing look.

I swallow the lump in my throat. Normally, yes, but not when there's a good chance I might be pregnant. But that's not something I want to explain out here on the road to my bizarre new neighbour. So instead, I just smile tightly.

'Good,' she says with finality, before turning around and walking back to her house. It's only when she's twenty feet away that I realise something.

'Sorry,' I call after her. 'I didn't catch your name.'

She turns back, her grip on the dog's lead unnervingly loose. 'My name's Maureen,' she says. 'No need to tell me yours – I already know. You're Imogen Blake and Patrick Cromford.'

With that, she gives a curt nod and disappears towards her cottage, Brutus trotting beside her.

Patrick and I stand in silence for a moment, still processing everything that has just happened. I stare at the empty gate where the pheasants hung only minutes ago, trying to reconcile the warm housewarming gift Maureen imagined with the grotesque display we've just witnessed.

'Well,' Patrick says after a beat, 'that was... something.'

I finally close my mouth, managing a dry laugh. 'Welcome to the countryside, I guess.'

Patrick shakes his head in disbelief, perhaps still holding the memory of the dead birds at arm's length. 'Seven o'clock stew,' he mutters, looking decidedly pale at the thought. 'What have we gotten ourselves into?'

I smile, but the weight of the day, with the interview, the key, the move, and Maureen's unsettling 'gift' sits heavy on my chest. It's just new house nerves, though. I'm sure it is. I'll feel better when we're all settled in.

7

'You can't tell me you don't feel just the slightest bit freaked out by that interaction,' I say as Patrick ushers us inside the house.

I glance out the window several times, but Maureen is nowhere to be seen. Still, a nervousness lingers in the pit of my stomach.

'It's just a different way of doing things,' he says. He takes me by the hand, although his gaze drifts outside. 'This is the countryside. Maybe it was a little forward of her to invite us to dinner on our first night, but I think she's just a lonely woman who wants some company. That's the impression I got. It's not like there are many other people near for her to talk to.'

'But the dead pheasants?' I ask. 'That's odd. You have to agree that's odd.'

'Is it, though? I mean, you wouldn't think twice about someone dropping off a lasagna, would you? Just because you can't see what animal the meat's from, it is still meat. Her gift was just a lot fresher than we're used to seeing.'

He's not wrong and the logical part of me agrees, but it doesn't ease the knot in my stomach entirely. Being able to anticipate how people are going to react is something I think I'm good at. It's something I try to be good at. I learned from a young age that knowing who you're dealing with can give you an edge. Clearly I don't know how country folk act or react yet and that makes me feel uncomfortable. Or at least unprepared.

'She knew our names. First and last,' I say, not yet ready to let the issue go. 'You don't think that's weird?'

He shrugs. 'There's probably only one estate agent that handles all the local villages and houses like this. My guess is she's badgered them enough to find out who we are. Sure, maybe she'll be a little irritating, but honestly? She's harmless. I can feel it.'

Patrick is usually a good judge of character. *Usually.* I put the modifier in there for Arabella, of course. And for Prim. But I've seen him call out plenty of people when he gets a bad vibe. People who've tried to offer us investment opportunities for my art – who I already knew were scammers – not to mention several realtors who tried their luck with places they wanted to convince us had 'incredible potential'. Maybe I should trust his instincts this time, too.

'You know,' he says, 'it could just be your hormones making you feel paranoid. That might be a good sign. We could always go up to London and do the blood test tomorrow rather than wait four more days. What do you think?'

What do I think? Do I want to know if I'm pregnant? Absolutely. But even after all the prodding and poking I've endured during the past four months of IVF treatment, it still gets to me. The only difference between this blood test and the others is that I don't *have* to do it. I don't need to put myself through that right now. Waiting a few more days and going for the standard peeing on a stick method is the best option – for my mental health, at least.

I shake my head. 'No, I don't want to go for the blood test. Definitely not after all that with the pheasants.' I let out a groan. 'Do we really have to go over there tonight?'

'Look.' He squeezes my hands gently. 'She's an old lady. I can't imagine she'll be here for that much longer. Not being so isolated and everything.'

'So you're saying we just have to wait it out until she dies?' I say, somewhat shocked by my husband's remark.

He laughs. 'I was actually thinking about when she moves into a nursing home.'

That makes more sense, but it still doesn't make me feel any less uneasy. I didn't expect to move into my new house and immediately start a countdown to when the neighbours left.

'How about this?' Patrick tries. 'We go there for dinner tonight, spend half an hour or so there, and then tomorrow, I'll start clearing out the outbuilding and setting up your art studio.'

'I thought I'd do that when you're in London for work,' I reply.

'I know,' he says, a mischievous smile curling at the corner of his lips. 'But think how much quicker it'll be with both of us doing it. So, what do you think? One meal at Mo's?'

'Mo's?' I said, once again offering him a questioning glare.

'I'm sure that's what people close to her call her.'

'Well, that is not going to be us. Hear me, you're not to accept any more dinner invitations from Mo without checking with me first. Got it?' Rather than reply, he seems to drift off for a moment. 'Patrick, are you listening?' I say, swinging my hand to playfully punch his arm, but before I can make contact, he grabs my wrist and pulls me into him.

'I love you, Imogen Blake,' he says softly, his lips brushing my forehead. 'And we are going to have the most wonderful future in this house. I can feel it.'

My eyes close involuntarily as I breathe in his familiar scent: the soft, musky aroma that always calms me and draws out the tension from my body.

'How did I get so lucky to marry you?' I murmur, feeling the warmth of his embrace.

'I guess it must've been fate,' he says, moving to kiss me, only for a loud horn to blare from outside.

I pull away, a grin spreading across my face for the first time all morning. 'I guess that must be the movers.'

8

At ten to seven, the house is in better order than I'd expected it to be. We've already unpacked all the obvious items – clothes are in the wardrobes, kitchenware is in the kitchen, furniture like tables and chairs are in the assigned rooms.

There are still plenty of boxes, though. All of my art supplies, to start with. They are piled high in the dining room, next to the patio doors. That way, when the studio is ready, we can take them straight outside, but that's not going to happen tonight. Not when we have somewhere else to be.

'I don't have anything to take round to Maureen's,' I say to Patrick as I slip on my shoes, ready to leave. 'I should've brought flowers or something. Maybe I should just take wine, anyway? I know she said not to, but I have to bring something, don't I?'

Patrick shakes his head. 'She won't expect anything like that. She knows we've just moved in. Honestly.'

'It's not about what she's expecting – it's about good manners. You shouldn't turn up at a house empty-handed.'

The idea of showing up at someone's home with a gift, be it wine, chocolates, or flowers, wasn't something I grew up with. If there was a bottle of wine in our house, my mum would've drunk it long before she considered giving it to anyone. But during my second year at art college, a tutor invited a few of us over. Out of the five students, I was the only one who showed up empty-handed.

'I didn't realise we were supposed to bring something...' I said to another student who was standing beside me with a bottle of rosé in their hand. 'She didn't mention bringing anything, did she?'

'It's just good manners, isn't it?' he replied.

I'd always thought I had good manners – using 'please' and 'thank you', holding doors open – but I hadn't realised it extended to things like this. From that day on, I never showed up anywhere empty-handed. I even bring wine to my own exhibitions, just in case we need an extra bottle – though I know Orla hates me doing that.

'Actually, if you're that concerned, why don't you bring one of your little sketches?' Patrick says.

'My sketches?'

'Yeah, everyone loves those. They'd make a lovely gift. If you won't sell them, you might as well put them to use.'

I know exactly which sketches he means. As an artist, I mainly work on large canvases in oil paint. It's the type of art you'd find hanging in the reception area of fancy offices. That's why Patrick first came to my exhibition – to find pieces for his office. But before I start on a large canvas, I sketch out several ideas, just in ink and pencil. I've got a notebook full of my musings, not to mention dozens of smaller scraps. I'll keep refining them until I'm confident in the composition and only then will I begin the actual piece. Patrick has told me hundreds of times how he thinks I could have an exhibition of just those little ideas. He thinks people will be interested in seeing the process. He even suggested the idea to Orla, who wasn't totally against it, either. It's sweet, but he's my husband – he thinks everything I do is great – and she's my agent – she has to think everything I do is great. The fact she's never raised it again is probably a sign that the sketches should stay where they are, away from the public eye.

'I don't know,' I say, responding to his suggestion. 'She might not even like art. Or my art anyway.'

'It's not about her taste, it's about the fact that it would be a lovely gift,' he says. 'I think she'd appreciate the personal touch. Why don't you find something, and I can go around there now? That way you don't have to worry about taking time to find a piece you like.'

I'm not convinced. To start with, I can't imagine why Patrick wouldn't want to wait for me; I certainly wouldn't want to turn up at a stranger's house without him there, but then, she's an old woman and he's a well-built man and he's probably right in thinking that both of us being late won't give the best impression. Besides, even a lame gift is better than none.

'Okay, I'll grab one,' I tell him, before giving him a quick peck on his cheek. 'I'll try to be as quick as I can.'

9

While our house is what I'd call a family home – four bedrooms, two bathrooms, including the ensuite, and plenty of downstairs living space – Maureen's place looks like the quintessential country cottage. There is one decent-sized window next to the front door, and two smaller ones upstairs, giving a clear indication of how narrow the house is. It doesn't seem to extend far back either.

Just like Patrick suggested, I'm carrying one of my sketches. It's the refinement of an idea that had been playing on my mind for some time and has splashes of watercolour on top of the ink. While it's abstract, it always evokes a sense of the sea and water, not just because of the blue washes but also the rippling, horizontal brushstrokes and gradient of colours. I'd hoped to bring something with greens or oranges to mirror the tones of our surroundings, but this is all I could find in a rush. Beggars can't be choosers.

There's no gate on Maureen's driveway, so I walk straight up to the door.

'That's weird,' I say to myself as I approach the house.

There's a fire extinguisher sitting on the doorstep. I've never known anyone to keep one outside their house before. Then again, she's an old lady. I guess you think about things like that more when you're her age. I suspect she's the type of person who unplugs everything before she goes to bed, too.

It took longer than I expected to find the sketch, and I feel guilty for leaving Patrick to face her on his own, but as I raise my hand to knock on the door, that feeling is replaced by one of fear as before my knuckles even make contact with the wood, the growling starts.

With my heart racing, I jump back.

'Okay, I should have been expecting that,' I say, trying to steady my pulse as I remember the large greyhound from earlier in the day. With a deep breath in, I go to knock again and this time I actually see it through.

'Brutus, stop it!' Maureen's voice is almost as gravelly as the dog's bark. 'You won't be sleeping on the bed tonight!'

I wish Patrick was with me, just so I could see the look on his face at her comment. I can't imagine sharing a bed with any animal, let alone a dog that size. I'd be worried it'd roll over in the night and suffocate me. As I imagine the little old lady hidden beneath a mound of fur, the door swings open and there stands Maureen.

'Come in, come in. I've put the heating on. Don't want to waste it,' she says, motioning us inside.

I hurry in, closing the door behind us. In my head, I'd already imagined what Maureen's cottage would look like on the inside, which is basically the standard vision of an old lady's house: patterned carpets, fussy wallpaper, and lots of clutter like decorative plates or photos. Given Brutus's size and the size of the house, I also assumed it'd smell like wet dog. But when I step through the door, I'm pleasantly surprised. There are no ornamental plates or overwhelming clutter. The walls are clean and white, and there isn't a hint of dog smell in the air – the only scent is fresh paint. However, I do notice two more fire extinguishers: one on the windowsill and one just inside the door. There's no way I'll get through the entire evening without asking about them, but good manners dictate I hold off a bit longer.

'Well, come on through,' Maureen says, leading us further into the house. 'The stew's ready. Patrick's in there.'

'Oh, thank you. And this is for you,' I say, offering her the sketch. She takes it, sniffs in what I assume is a gesture of thanks, then carries on walking. Not an art fan then.

Like the living area, the kitchen-dining space is compact but clean and surprisingly modern. There's a new oven and a modern hob, although the fridge is tiny. I guess that makes sense for someone living on their own, especially if they're happy to eat whatever they catch out in the wild.

As I walk in, Patrick stands up from the table and moves over to me.

'Hey, are you okay?' he says, pulling me in close and hugging me tightly. From the way he holds my body to his, it's like we've been separated for days or weeks, not for half an hour.

'I'm fine,' I say, stepping back so I can look into his eyes. 'And you? How's your conversation been?'

'You'll want red wine with pheasant,' Maureen says, interrupting us before Patrick can say anything. My stomach plummets as she pulls three glasses from a cabinet.

I glance at Patrick. There's no way I'm drinking wine after everything I've been through with IVF treatment, but there's no way I'm telling her about the possible pregnancy either.

'Actually,' I say, 'I'm on antibiotics – pretty strong ones. I had a bad chest infection. I'm fine with just water.'

She gives me a look as if she's about to say something, but she puts the wine glass back and grabs a tumbler. I hear her mutter, 'No drink, no meat, no fun.'

'Can I help with anything?' I ask, trying to make up for the clearly poor impression I've made so far. But she shakes her head.

'No, no, everything's good,' she says, pulling out two bowls and moving over to the slow cooker. 'Now, I suppose you'll be wanting the lowdown on this place? Well, here's my first bit of advice. It's not safe. Not safe at all. You should sell up now and leave if you want to get out of here alive.'

10

Silence sweeps around the room as the hairs rise on the back of my neck. I swear I feel the blood drain from my face. I open my mouth, unsure if I even have the words to speak, when Maureen throws her head back and laughs.

'Oh, you should've seen your faces!' she gasps between cackles. 'Oh, that was a picture! I'm sorry, I'm sorry, but really... you looked like you'd seen a ghost!' She wipes her eyes, still giggling. 'You think a place like this is going to be less safe than the big city where you've come from? Don't be ridiculous.'

I glance at Patrick and it appears he's having as much trouble seeing the funny side of the joke as I am.

'Does anyone live in the cottage next to you?' I ask, feeling the need to take some control over the conversation, though I'm not entirely sure how much I trust Maureen not to wind me up with her answers.

'Not at the minute. Robbie lived there for the best part of a decade. Had a young wife too, but they packed off after Clarence. Didn't want to live so close to the house, I suppose. They found him, you see.'

'Found him? Clarence? Is he the person who owned our house before?'

'Aye, but he upset a quite few people. Dodgy dealings, see. Money problems. Got a fair few people up in Tarlton to invest and it all went tits up. People were mad. I don't know how much he took off them, but it was a lot. I know that much. I never 'ad any problems with him myself, but probably 'cause he knew there was no point tapping me up for any cash.' She grins in a way that makes me think she's going to let out another of her cackles, but her face falls again almost instantly. 'Guess he thought there was no way out. Sad, that. There's always a way out.'

I take a moment to absorb what Maureen has just told me. Not just about Clarence, but about her neighbours and the reason they left. From the clenching in my gut, I know exactly what she's alluded to, but I need to ask her outright. I need to know I'm not being paranoid.

'He killed himself? Clarence killed himself in our house?'

'Aye, he did,' she says quietly.

Once again, silence takes a hold. As I look at Patrick, a hundred thoughts roll through my head. A hundred questions that Maureen might well have the answer to. Like when did he do it, and in what room and how long was it until they found him? I need to know the answers, but I can't ask. Not without coming across as utterly insensitive and self-serving. Yet I need to say something. The temperature in the room is starting to drop and I don't know if it's real, or if it's because my mind doesn't want to process what's going on. Along with the vegetarianism and lack of drinking, I think a panic attack would be the last nail in the coffin for Maureen and me, and so I ask the only question I can think of.

'The fire extinguishers,' I say, turning my head and looking at the one on the windowsill. 'How come you have so many of them? Did something happen?'

Maureen's eyes follow mine as if she hadn't known the object was there. After a moment, she lets out a slight laugh, but unlike the previous cackles, this one is closer to a scoff.

'Oh, yes, something happened,' she said. 'The kids up at Springfield Farm. They're what happened.'

11

'The fires?' I ask, feeling a knot tighten in my stomach.

For the first time all evening, Maureen's confidence falters. Even when she was talking about Clarence's death, she remained incredibly matter of fact. But this is different. She looks down at Brutus, who lies quietly by her feet. I may have laughed at Patrick's comment about getting a guard dog earlier, not to mention the idea that Maureen lets Brutus sleep in her bed, but clearly there are reasons she has a dog like him. She's on her own, and Brutus is her protection.

'I mean, it was just kids being kids,' she says with a sigh. 'Around here, there's not much for them to do. No skate parks, no cinemas, nothing really. So last year, they took to burning things.'

I swallow the lump that's lodged in my throat. 'Burning things?'

'At first, it was nothing to worry about. Old car tyres, fallen-down trees – anything they could get their hands on, really. But then they started coming into people's gardens. One evening, they set fire to the rose bushes at Cedar Lodge. It's about a mile down the road, just outside of Tarlton. Lovely house. Lovely rose bushes, too. Used to be, anyway. I guess after the village, they wanted to try somewhere a little more secluded. I reckon they thought they could do bigger things that way too.'

'Here?' I say. 'Did they set fire to the house?'

Maureen shakes her head. 'My house, no, but my shed.'

A new chill fills the air as Maureen draws in a long breath. I don't need to persuade her to carry on with her story. I can see it in her eyes. She wants to tell us.

'It was about eight months ago now. No, I tell a lie. It was nine. Nights were still dark, you see. I'd gone to bed early – no point staying up unless there's something on television. I'm not one for company that often.' She smiles at this remark and I can see that once again, Patrick was right. The old woman just wanted some company. 'I'd been sound asleep when Brutus started barking like mad, running up and down the stairs, nipping at me. It wasn't normal. When I looked out the window, there it was – my shed, lit up like a Guy on Bonfire Night.' Her voice falters for a moment.

'I'm so sorry,' I say. I know the words aren't enough, but it's not like I can sit here and say nothing. Once again, Maureen offers a flicker of a smile.

'Yeah, well, I got out, called the fire brigade. They came and put it out, and I was lucky. It didn't reach the house. Could've been a lot worse, but I can still smell it, you know? Everything smelled like smoke. Maybe it was just in my head, but still... I 'ad a painter round to freshen things up, but he said he couldn't smell a thing. Suggested I light some candles.' She scoffs. 'Candles, really?' She pauses, then shrugs. 'So yeah, I'm a bit paranoid now. Got fire extinguishers all over the place. Been trained on how to use them too, but I haven't needed to. Yet.'

I expect Patrick to ask something, as I feel like I've been

dominating the conversation with my questions, but he remains silent, and so I ask the next one that's whirring around my mind. 'Did they go to prison? The kids?'

Maureen lets out a scoff. 'Prison? You think anyone connected to Springfield Farm would ever see the inside of a prison cell? Most of the village is related to them in one way or another. Donny tried his best to make something stick, though.'

'Donny?' Patrick suddenly joins in. I don't feel like she's said the name before either, but I could be wrong.

'Aye, Donny. Lives up in Tarlton. He's some big police detective or something. Chief inspector maybe? Oh, I don't know. He tried his best, but no, they didn't go to prison. Still, I haven't heard of any fires in about nine months now, so maybe whatever he did or said scared them off. Then again, maybe they've grown out of it.'

'That's awful,' I say. 'I'm so sorry you had to go through that.'

Maureen smiles slightly. 'Well, you can't have it all perfect, can you?' She squares her shoulders, as if shaking off the weight of the memories. 'And everything else about this place is as a dream. At least, when spring comes, it is.'

I reach out my hand for my glass of water, wishing I could actually have wine. Local arsonists and a house with a past are not what you want to hear on the first day of a fresh start.

12

'That was a lot to take in in one night,' I say as Patrick and I remove our coats. He had been unusually quiet over dinner, but given the time with Maureen that he'd had to endure on his own, I couldn't really blame him. Now we're back though, but it's clear that some of the things she said are still playing on his mind.

As I slip off my shoes, my eyes land naturally in the living room. Is that where Clarence did it? Is that where the former owner took their life? I doubt it. It doesn't feel like the type of room that someone would do something like that in. But then, nowhere in this house does, and I would have thought I, above all people, had a better sense of things like that than most. 'I thought they had to disclose suicides?' I say, moving my gaze from the living room to the dining room. 'I thought estate agents had to tell perspective owners if that had happened.'

'I don't know what to tell you,' Patrick says, squeezing my hand. 'You know I'd never have considered it if I'd have known. Not after what happened to you. I'm sorry for this.'

'You don't need to apologise,' I say, kicking my shoes off. 'I read all the paperwork, too. I didn't see anything.'

'So you think Maureen was lying?'

I hadn't thought that at all, and even with Patrick putting the idea into my head, I can't believe it.

'Why would she make that up? She wouldn't gain anything. And she's obviously paranoid about the fires. No one would have that many extinguishers otherwise.'

'So what do you want to do?' he asks, his brow crinkled in concern.

'About what?'

'About the house. Are you okay staying here? You know, with everything? Do you want to move?'

There's no point pretending the thought of packing everything straight back into a removal van hasn't cross my mind, but the truth is, if you buy an old house then it's going to have some history to it, and not all of it is going to be pleasant. Of course, this news is a little more recent history than I would have liked.

'We'll just have to make it our own,' I say with all the conviction I can muster. 'We'll cancel out all the negative memories with positive ones.'

'That sounds like a perfect idea,' Patrick says, pulling me in and kissing me. 'Now, what do you say to a decaf coffee? I'll make it. You go put your feet up.'

'That sounds like a perfect idea.'

Once Patrick has made the drinks, we sit on the sofa and continue to talk about the meal with Maureen.

'I can't believe kids around here would set fire to an old woman's shed,' I say. 'I didn't think that type of thing would happen somewhere like this.'

'Somewhere wealthy, you mean?'

'I guess.'

Patrick shrugs. 'Kids are kids, and like Maureen said, there's not a lot for them to do here. I did pretty dumb things when I was young and bored, too.'

I raise an eyebrow. 'Surely not perfect, law-abiding Patrick, destined for a legal career? I can't believe you ever put a toe out of line growing up.'

He laughs again. 'Not when I knew I wanted to be a lawyer, no. But before that? Let's just say I did a few things I'm not proud of.'

My eyebrow stays arched. We've spent a lot of time talking about our pasts, but while I tend to share things from my early life – about my mum and growing up – Patrick mostly talks about his more recent life. I know how Arabella changed when she had Prim and how, when Prim started acting up, they sent her to boarding school, hoping it would straighten her out. Spoiler: it didn't. But teenage Patrick? I've always pictured him as a mini version of the man standing in front of me now.

'So, what kind of things did you get up to?' I ask, intrigued. 'What's the worst thing you've ever done?'

He gives me a playful smile. 'Okay, promise you won't judge me?'

I shift back, teasingly pulling out of his reach. 'Now I have to know.'

He takes a deep breath and then lets it out. 'I stole something.'

'Stole what?' My heart pounds, and I'm desperate to hear what my goody-goody, law-abiding husband has done.

'A Discman.'

I blink, trying not to laugh. 'A Discman? Like a portable CD player?'

'Yes, one of those,' he says, the guilt from years ago still etched across his face.

I can't stop myself. 'Wow, I'm shocked! Not because you stole something, but because you're old enough to have used a Discman.'

'Hey!' Patrick laughs. 'It wasn't that long ago. Everyone at school had one, but I didn't. There was this small shop about half a mile from where we lived. It sold everything. Toys, electronics, and it had barely any security, so... well, I pinched it.'

I press my lips together in the hope of stopping myself from laughing, but I can't. This shop-lifting character is just so far from the Patrick I know and love, it's impossible not to find the story ridiculous. 'So what did you do? Did you keep it?'

'No, I couldn't even bring myself to open the box. It sat under my bed for two days before I returned it.' He shakes his head, clearly still carrying the weight of his teenage guilt.

'That's so you,' I say, imagining a younger version of Patrick sneaking the Discman back into the shop. 'Why didn't you just ask your parents for one? Birthday or Christmas?'

He shrugs. 'I could've, I guess. But my parents weren't great at listening, and I wasn't great at talking to them. Anyway, it's in the past now. But I promise you our little one will never have to shoplift for a Discman. Or anything else, for that matter.' He places a hand on my stomach.

'I don't think they even make them any more. Besides...' I hesitate. 'We don't even know if there's a little one in there yet.'

Patrick gives me a reassuring smile. 'If not now, there will be soon. Now, let's get to bed. I've got some art studio clearing to do tomorrow, right?'

'Sounds good,' I say. 'If you check the downstairs windows, I'll do the upstairs ones. Then we can head to bed.'

'You do realize we're in the middle of nowhere?' he asks, tilting his head to the side.

'I do,' I reply, 'but I also know there are a bunch of pyromaniac teens running around and you never know who might try their luck.'

'Don't worry, I'm on it,' he says, before kissing me softly on the lips.

As I head upstairs, I hear Patrick securing the back door. I know we're probably safer here than we've ever been in the city, but old habits die hard. My mum may not have taught me much about etiquette, but she sure drilled into me to always check that the doors and windows are locked.

There are three windows at the front of the house and three at the back. I start with the front, stepping into what I hope will become the nursery if everything goes well. As I switch on the light, I take a moment to look around, imagining the room filled with a crib and a changing table. I picture a little chalkboard where our child can draw once they're old enough to hold a pencil. I know Patrick would say I'm getting ahead of myself, but I can't help it.

The curtains are thick, flocked fabric left by the previous owners. Clarence. A shudder trickles down my spine. Maybe this is the room he chose to do the deed in, I think, before swallowing back the thought. I can't fixate on what happened here. If I do, I'll go insane and I know exactly what that feels like. I don't plan on keeping the curtains – they're far from suitable for a nursery. I'll get online tomorrow and order some more. Still, whether or not I want to keep them doesn't change the fact that I need to close them now, yet as I reach for the fabric, something outside catches my eye.

The fields have been harvested since our last visit and the lack of crops means the view stretches even further across the rolling hills. Pinprick lights glimmer from the nearest village while the silhouettes of trees stand bold and black, far closer to home. I turn my head, assuming it was a moving branch that caught my attention. But as I stare out into the watery moonlight, something moves again and my stomach lurches. Even with the lack of light, I know exactly what I'm looking at, and it's not a tree. Someone is out there, staring up at my house. Staring up at me.

13

'It was probably a culmination from all the stress you've had to deal with over the last couple of days,' Patrick says. 'You know how your imagination can make you see things when you're on edge.'

I don't warrant his comment with a remark. The moment I yelled his name, Patrick raced up the stairs to find me white and trembling, and yet when he looked out at the view, the figure had gone. For twenty minutes we waited there, but there was nothing other than one swooping owl and a prowling fox. Eventually, he persuaded me to get into bed. But going to bed and going to sleep are very different things.

'You said yourself you couldn't even tell if it was a man or woman. It could have been a deer. They're about the same height as a person.'

'They also have four legs,' I say, my unease shifting to annoyance. 'It was a person, and they were watching me. I could feel it.'

With a slight rub of his temples, Patrick rolls over in bed, props himself up on one elbow, and looks me in the eye. 'Im, this is a huge change. The house, the baby, not to mention some of the things Maureen said today. It's only natural to feel nervous. *I'm* feeling nervous.'

'You are?'

'Of course I am.'

I'm sure he expected his words to calm me, but they're doing anything but.

'What are you feeling nervous about?' I say. 'You think it was a mistake moving out this far? Or the baby? Are you nervous about the baby? We talked about this. You said you wanted to do this?'

He takes my hand, at the same time as tucking a strand of hair behind my ear.

'No, I am not nervous about this baby. Not in the slightest, or the house, but there's going to be an adjustment period. Like the commute. I'm worried that some days I'll still have to work late or stay in London, and you'll be all the way out here on your own. I'm worried about how long it's going to take to get your studio up and running, because I know you need to be painting to be happy and we've no idea what state that outbuilding is in. And I'm nervous about how Prim is going to adapt to the idea of having a half-sister. So, yeah, there are things I'm nervous about, too.'

The last thing I needed was a reminder of Prim and how she has a key to the house. Would it be too much to wish that if the arsonists turn up, it will be when Patrick and I are out and she's paying us a surprise visit? I quickly quash the thought. Prim's Patrick's daughter and I'd never want anything bad to happen to her, merely because of the effect it would have on him.

'I also think we need to take whatever Maureen says with a pinch of salt,' Patrick says, interrupting my thoughts. 'She's an old woman who lives on her own. When you're alone, things can seem bigger and scarier. That's just how it is.'

'I understand what you're saying. I really do.' I stress my words as much as I can. 'But that doesn't change the fact that there was someone out there. I'm positive someone was looking into the house.'

'Then maybe it was a poacher,' Patrick concedes. 'Someone out hare coursing. Or just a nosey neighbour from one of the nearby villages out for an evening stroll. This is the first time the house has had lights on inside it for months. They might have just been curious and trying to work out who's moved in. Or wanted to say hi, even. Just like Maureen and her pheasant "gift". You thought *that* was a threat, remember?'

He's right. Maybe I wouldn't have called it a threat exactly, but I definitely assumed it was some kind of sick joke, and I was wrong.

Patrick leans forward and kisses me gently on the forehead. 'Come on, you need a proper night's sleep. Fingers crossed, by the end of tomorrow you'll have your art studio.'

The niggling unease continues to gripe at me, but everything he's said has made perfect sense. This is what you get in the countryside: dead animals and people wandering around at all hours. Perhaps it's not the type of place I'd envision my child growing up in, after all. Assuming I'm pregnant, that is. Only three days until I can do the test and find out.

14

'Now *this* is why we moved here,' Patrick says as we stand outside in the garden, holding mugs of steaming coffee in our hands. Even after the rough night's sleep, it's hard to disagree. The air has that crisp autumn feeling – chilly but not cold – and there's not so much as a single cloud in the sky. Nothing but miles and miles of bright clear blue. The whole atmosphere is completely serene, which is a stark contrast to last night. I don't know if it's rats, or mice or birds nesting in our roof, but I swear something is in there and was scratching until the early hours. Not that Patrick heard at all. No, his snoring ensured a perfect night's rest for him. In the end I had to dig out my earplugs to block out the noises – both Patrick's and the animals' – but that won't be a long-term solution. We can't have rats in a house with a baby, but I guess that's something we can deal with nearer the time. And like Patrick says, a morning like this is all it takes to make the night before feel like a distant memory.

I breathe in a lungful of air and feel it hit my lungs. It's the perfect temperature for going for a cycle ride, which was what I tried to do first thing, but Patrick was insistent that I help him sort the studio so he knows where everything should go.

That's just an excuse, of course. He's worried about me going cycling on the country roads on my own, but I'm going to do it at some point. Choosing a day like today, before the weather changes, seems like a sensible thing to do. Particularly when I already know he won't let me lift any of the boxes in the outbuilding. It was the same yesterday when the lorry arrived. I just had to look on and direct him and the removal men. Still, tomorrow he's going to head back to work and I want to make the most of the time with him. Even if that time is spent sorting out someone else's belongings.

The outbuilding is about thirty feet from the house and around the size of a double garage. Like most of the cottages and homes around here, it's made from yellow-coloured bricks, while long windows are opaque with dirt. The only door is metal, warped *and* rusted; however, the padlock is firmly in place.

'Now, where are the bolt cutters?'

Bolt cutters and Patrick weren't something I'd ever imagined together. But when the estate agent showed us around, they mentioned how cutting off the padlock would be the easiest way to get inside. Patrick didn't tell me he was buying the cutters – he just came home with them the evening after we'd had the offer accepted, and he's been holding on to them ever since, waiting for this moment.

'Do you actually know what you're doing with those?' I ask, raising an eyebrow.

'They're just like big scissors, right?' he says, positioning the cutters around the rusted padlock. He glances at me. 'Maybe step back a bit, just in case.'

I take a few steps back, and moments later, there's a loud *clink* as the padlock drops to the ground.

'Told you so,' he says with a wide grin.

As I move forward, Patrick places his hand around the handle. From the decades' worth of rust, I assume it'll take some force to get it open, but he offers one sharp tug, and it swings wide.

'Well,' he says, stepping aside to let me see in. 'You're going to have *a lot* of space once we start clearing it out.'

I hang back for a moment. 'Any sign of dead mice? Or live ones, for that matter?'

He laughs. 'No, just a lot of boxes and dust. And... shelves packed with stuff.'

Confident there's nothing too gross in there, I peer inside cautiously before taking a step inward. He wasn't joking about me having space. I knew from the outside it was big, but I don't think I appreciated how big until now. I stand there envisioning the setup. Where I will place my easel, my canvases, my drying area. There's a sink already in here, which is a bonus I hadn't expected. With London prices at such a premium, I've always been limited by how big my work could go. This changes that. The itch to get going is greater than ever and I move further in.

The grime coating the windows is so thick that barely any natural light gets through. The brooding atmosphere would have been a perfect backdrop to create my old style of work, but I've made a concerted effort to move away from that into something more – what was it the journalist called it? – mainstream and uplifting. Uplifting requires light. Thankfully, as I stare in through the dimness, I spot a string hanging from the ceiling and tug on it. An overhead strip light flickers a few times before settling and casting the room in its harsh glow. It's not an ideal light to paint by, but I can deal with it for now.

'We'll need to hire a skip,' I say to Patrick as I pull myself out of my daydreams. Right now, there's not even space to put my materials, and I'm the type of person who can't think in clutter. 'Either that or we'll be filling the dustbin for the next three years.'

Patrick nods. 'I guess it depends on what's in these boxes. Some of it might be worth selling. Or at least donating.'

He's right. This is an affluent area, and while we don't *need* the money, I've never been one to pass up a good opportunity.

'Okay,' I say. 'I guess we should start looking.'

The boxes aren't taped shut, just folded over. I open the first one, and Patrick does the same.

'What've you got?' he asks.

'Looks like tools – jewellery-making stuff, maybe. What about you?'

'Wire,' he says, raising an eyebrow. 'Wire and clay, I think.'

'They were definitely some sort of craftsperson,' I say as I move on to the next box. 'Maybe I'll sort through it later and see if any local artists are interested. If I don't want them, that is.'

We move quickly through the next few boxes, which hold more of the same. But when I reach the third one, something feels different. It's larger than the others, heavier. I've got a strange feeling this box holds the key to what the former occupant used this space for.

Without hesitation, I pull the top open – and freeze. My hand flies to my mouth.

'Im, what is it? What have you found?'

I don't speak. I can't. My entire body refuses to respond as a pair of lifeless eyes stare up at me.

15

I stumble back. My heart races. Rushing blood whirs behind my ears. Even though I squeeze my eyelids shut, I can still see those blank eyes staring out at me from the box. Crystal blue and unblinking. I know exactly what I just saw. Dead eyes. Something dead is inside that box.

'Imogen!' Patrick races over to me. 'What is it? What did you find?'

'There's something in there.' My voice is shaking. 'Something... It's dead. I don't know. I don't know what it is.'

'It's okay, it's okay.' He places a hand on my chest gently while stretching his body out to peer into the box I just opened, although he can't see much. He's too far away to look inside it. As he turns back to face me, he squeezes my shoulders before releasing me entirely. 'It's all right. You just stay there, okay? You're fine, you'll be absolutely fine. You stay where you are. I'll handle it.'

Even as he moves away from me, he keeps repeating himself. His soft voice is normally so soothing, but I can't block out what I've just seen. I keep replaying it in my mind, over and over. *Was it a person?* No. I shake the thought away. I would've smelled something, wouldn't I? Surely we would have smelt *something* when we opened the door. But all dead creatures smell, not just people, so what the hell was it?

'Well, I know what the former occupant's hobby was, at least,' Patrick says. I look at him and find him smiling, as if the whole thing is amusing.

'What the hell is it?' My voice is close to a shout.

He reaches into the box and pulls the object out. The first thing I see is a wooden base, then what looks like red fur. But it's only when he tilts it towards me and those bright blue eyes flash again that I understand what I'm looking at.

'A fox? It's a dead fox?' My stomach lurches as I stare at the creature, dust coated and dead, but perfectly preserved.

'Yep,' Patrick replies, still calm. 'I guess the former occupant was a taxidermy fan. That's what all the tools are for. It makes sense why I found a bottle full of glass eyes earlier.'

I shake my head, trying to ease the queasiness that has taken hold, but all I can do is look at the boxes. We've opened barely a quarter of them and judging by the jar of glass eyes Patrick mentioned, the fox probably isn't the only finished exhibit in here. 'Do you think there are more?' I ask.

'I don't know.'

We stand there in silence when a sudden buzzing makes me jump. 'It's my phone,' Patrick says, putting the fox down before pulling his phone from his pocket. 'It's just my phone.' After a quick glance at the screen, he frowns. 'It's work. I'll call them back later.' He ends the call, then walks towards me and places his hands on my arms. I'm still in the exact same place I was a moment a go. It's funny. So often you think you'll run when something scares you, but I guess adrenaline is called the fight, flight, or freeze hormone for a reason, and I already know I'm the type of person who freezes.

'Look, it's fine. I'll deal with this,' Patrick says. 'I'm sure there's a local taxidermy company that'll take the lot. You don't need to worry about it. Why don't you go inside, sit down for a minute? I'll come with you. I'll make you a drink.'

As my legs feel like jelly, and my heart won't stop pounding, I put most of my weight on Patrick as he leads me into the house, though even when I'm sitting in the kitchen, my hands continue to tremble.

'I'm so sorry, Im. I should've checked first. I don't know why I let you in there with me while I went through all that stuff.'

'You didn't *let* me. I wanted to be in there. It's going to be my studio. I should be the one to clear it out. I just... I didn't think people still did that. Do they really still do that?'

'I guess they do.'

My throat is so dry it hurts to swallow, but I can't stomach the thought of eating or drinking anything right now. Still, I can't help but chuckle at the irony; I'd been hoping for some nausea in the next few days, but from a successful implantation, not from seeing a bunch of dead animals.

'Do you think there's a chance we're just not cut out for country life?' I say as Patrick hands me a cup of tea.

He laughs gently before kissing me on the lips. 'We're absolutely cut out for it. It's just going to take some time, that's all. It's been a pretty rough start, with the pheasants and now this...'

'Yeah, you're right.'

My romantic vision of country living had been evenings by the fire; walks through wildflower fields or frost-covered woods. So far, it's been death, an eccentric neighbour and news of troubled teens causing havoc.

'Don't worry. I'll take care of everything in there,' Patrick says. 'You just relax.'

'Relax?' I scoff. 'I'm not exactly sure how to do that right now. Unless... Maybe I should go for a ride.'

'A bike ride? Are you sure you're up for it?'

I nod. 'Yes, I think I need it. I'll just go into town. It's four miles, right? I'll head there, have a wander, then come back. Hopefully, that'll give you enough time to deal with the fox and whatever friends he's got in those boxes.'

I think he's about to object. Maybe suggest I stay here and rest. But I'm willing to fight him on it. I need this. Thankfully, he nods.

'Okay, just make sure your phone's charged. I want to be able to get hold of you.'

'Of course,' I reply. 'And thank you, Patrick.'

At this, he shakes his head.

'You don't have to thank me. You're my wife. We're a team. And I know you'd do the same for me.'

'Move dead animals? I'm not sure I would.'

He laughs. 'Oh, a couple of years of countryside living and you might surprise yourself.'

'Hmm. I'm not so sure about that.'

'Well, I'll love you either way. Now, you better get going. I've got a load of dead animals to deal with.'

16

It's pretty much a straight road from our house to the town. Okay, *straight* isn't the right word; it's winding and narrow, like most of the roads around here, and let's not forget the hills. But there are only a couple of crossroads that I just have to go straight over, which is a relief. It means I don't have to keep my phone mounted on the handlebars, and I'm not a fan of cycling like that. Especially not when I need to keep both eyes on the road.

It only takes a few minutes for my muscles to relax into the motion of pedalling and for the first time in twenty-four hours, I actually feel like myself. I wouldn't go as far as to say I feel *relaxed* – there are still several layers of tension buzzing around in the back of my mind. The silhouette in the darkness is one of them. Prim is another. And then there's the obvious issue of how Patrick is going to get rid of those horrific items. But the worries are subdued for now, overridden by the fresh air rushing over my face and arms and the burn that is settling into my thighs as I weave down these quiet country lanes.

Switching off is not something I can do. Ever. The only time my mind really quiets is when I'm painting. When I'm focused on moving my hand with just the right pressure, mixing the perfect tone, using just enough paint to get the texture I want. Painting isn't just how I make a living; it's how I keep myself feeling safe. So it's no real surprise that I've been feeling stressed these last couple of days. Thankfully, I can already tell that this ride is going to reduce that by a little.

I got the bike a couple of years before I met Patrick. I didn't travel far or often enough in London to justify the expense of owning a car, but there were moments, especially on sunny days, when I couldn't stand the thought of cramming into a Tube carriage, inhaling a hundred different variations of body odour as I struggled to maintain an inch of personal space. Buses were just as bad, but taxis were still a luxury I couldn't justify using every day. So when I spotted a second-hand bike going for a good price, it felt like fate was nudging me. There was just one small problem: the only bike I knew how to ride was in a spin class.

Another item to add to the long list of things my mother never taught me.

Maybe it's wrong to keep a tally of her failings as a parent. I mean, at least I still think of her as a parent, which is more than I can say for my father. The only thing I have from him is his DNA. I don't even know his name, and I don't want to. He knew about me and was there for only two months of my life. After that, he decided my mother and I weren't worth the trouble. Maybe he was right about her, but not me. Every parent should know their children if they're given that luxury. In my opinion, anyway.

For the first month after learning to ride, I barely used the Tube. Of course, that changed when winter came, but on days when I needed inspiration, I'd hop on the bike and cycle around the parks regardless of how cold or wet it was. I loved it. It gave me a sense of freedom, of being connected to the world around me. But that feeling doesn't compare to this one. Because here, I'm not confined to cycle paths in a park or single-lane streets cluttered with traffic lights. Here, I can keep going. One country lane after another, with nothing to stop me.

After about fifteen minutes of cycling, only three cars have passed me – one coming towards me and two from behind. The roads are narrow, but there's plenty of room for them to pass, and any nerves I had have long gone.

I reach a crossroads and spot an old wooden signpost pointing to the town. One more mile to go. Just as I'd said to Patrick, this is the perfect way to calm myself, and I don't feel like I've stressed my body – or the possible baby – at all.

I stop at the crossroads, checking both ways to make sure nothing's coming. The visibility is clear, and I'm ready to move again when suddenly I hear the low growl of an engine. I twist my head over my shoulder to gauge how far away the car is, but it's almost on top of me – speeding too fast to stop.

One thought and one thought alone fills my mind: it's going to hit me. The car is going to hit me.

17

My body slams into the hedgerow as my mind scrambles to make sense of what just happened. The car – it's gone. It raced away, speeding straight through the crossroads without so much as a horn blast, not even bothering to check for oncoming traffic. I don't know how I managed it, but somehow, I threw myself into the hedge at the last second.

Standing up, I feel a sharp sting along my elbow. I glance down and see it's covered in scratches and bruises.

'Shit,' I mutter, tugging on the bike handlebars, only to find them tangled in brambles. 'Shit, shit, shit.'

After a couple of yanks, I free it, but I don't move to get on. Instead, I pull my phone from my pocket. So much for cycling into town – my best bet now is to call Patrick and get him to pick me up. Only... there's not even a flicker of reception.

'Shit, shit, *shit*.'

I look up at the signpost. Cirencester is only a mile away, and I've already cycled at least three times that far. Do I turn around and head home or push on for the extra mile? Going back home now will make the entire ride feel like a failure and do nothing to ease Patrick's paranoia. As such, it's an easy decision to make; keep going. The country lanes should open into wider roads soon enough, and hopefully, there'll be no more lunatic drivers. Plus, I can get a coffee, ring Patrick and ask him to pick me up.

I glance over at my bike and give it a quick once-over. Somehow, it appears to have gotten away without so much as a scratch. Trying to ignore the shakiness in my legs, I get back on and continue.

My knowledge of Cirencester extends to it being a small market town with an abbey and a few supermarkets on the outskirts. It's hardly much to go on, but as I cycle in, I can already tell I'll like it. It's quaint. Charming and full of character. It's the kind of town where I could definitely imagine running an art class, at least before the baby comes along. At the thought of our possible child, my heart tightens. When I came off the bike, I didn't fall on my stomach, did I? No. No, I didn't fall hard at all. I landed at an angle, caught by the hedge. Any of the force landed on my shoulder. That couldn't have hurt it, could it?

As soon as the thought forms, the icy chill of an incoming panic attack spreads along my arms. God, of all the places for this to happen, cycling down a road has to be one of the worst. I press hard on the brakes, then stop alongside the pavement, using my foot to balance me. As I close my eyes, I draw in a long, deep breath.

'You're safe,' I say to myself quietly. 'You are safe here. Patrick is safe. You are safe. Just breathe.'

When people look at my artwork, they usually say one of two things: either 'Oh my goodness, you're so talented,' or 'Wow, you must've worked really hard to get this good.' The second group has a better grip on reality, but no one ever says the truth. No one ever looks at my art and says, 'Wow, your panic attacks must've been so bad that you were scared to leave the house, so you threw yourself into art as an escape from reality.' Maybe they've thought it but good manners dictated they kept it to themselves. I doubt it, though.

But I don't need to escape reality now. My reality is good. If there is an embryo growing inside me then that fall would not have hurt it, and if not – if this round of IVF didn't work – we'll try again. And if that doesn't work, we'll find another way.

I feel my body temperature stabilise as I grip the bike's handlebars. I spot a sign for parking and head that way, pulling my phone out to call Patrick. It rings twice before he picks up.

'Hey, gorgeous! How's it going? Is it nice there?'

'Actually,' I say, 'I was wondering if you could come and get me? I had a bit of an accident on the way.'

'What do you mean?' His voice hitches an octave higher. 'An accident? Are you okay? Do you need to go to the hospital?'

'No, nothing like that. It's just... a car, some big Land Rover thing, ran me into the hedgerow.'

'*What?*' His fear turns to fury. 'Did you get the plate number? We need to go to the police. I'm sure there's a station in town. You need to report this now.'

I shake my head, even though he can't see me. 'No, I didn't. I didn't see the plate. It was green, and I think it was a Land Rover. That's all I've got. I'm fine, honestly – just a few scratches. I just wondered if you could pick me up. That's why I was calling. I don't really feel like cycling back.'

I expect him to agree right away. It hadn't actually crossed my mind that he wouldn't. So when there's a pause, I know something's up.

'Patrick. What is it? Where are you?'

He lets out a slight sigh. 'Well, I was sorting out the taxidermy stuff. I found a guy online who said he'd take it, but I have to deliver it to him, so I packed up all the animals and boxes I could fit in the car and went. It made sense at the time. You know, I just wanted to get them out of there for you.'

'Right...' I force a smile into my voice. 'It *does* make sense. It's fine, really.'

'Are you sure? You can wait there and I'll pick you up when I'm done, but I'll be a few hours. This guy's in Oxford.'

'Oxford?' I echo, trying to gauge how far that is. I know it's not just down the road.

'Like I said, I thought it was best to get rid of everything as soon as possible.'

'You're right. You're doing the right thing. Thank you for dealing with it.' I take a breath. 'Don't worry about me. I'll grab a coffee and then cycle back.'

'Are you sure you'll be all right? Why don't you get a taxi? You could put the bike in the back of it.'

'That's a good idea, but I'll see how I'm feeling when I'm ready to leave,' I say.

'All right. Just be careful, okay? I love you.'

'I love you too.' I hang up, trying to quash the small wave of disappointment. Patrick and I have never been the type of couple who need to do everything together. He was in a marriage like that with Arabella, and it nearly broke him, so I've always prided myself on being different, understanding when he has things to do.

Besides, he's doing this for *me*. I can't be annoyed at him for that. As for the taxi suggestion, it's a good one. Only if I don't cycle back, what's that telling my subconscious? That it's not safe? That I shouldn't cycle around here? I know better than most the strength of the subconscious, and I refuse to knowingly give mine that type of power. I guess I'll just have to wait and see how I feel in an hour or so.

I pull a small lock from my rucksack and lock my bike up to

the nearest rail. In London, I wouldn't have dared leave it with just this, but there's a farmer's market next door and a gift shop close by. It feels safe.

As I stand up, I scan the area and decide which way to go for coffee. Yet before I move, I notice someone by the wall. Something about the person reminds me of the figure I saw last night, the one watching me through the curtains from the green. It's the same pose, the same aura.

And I'm sure they're staring right at me. Poacher or nosey neighbour, my arse. I think I'm being followed.

18

I was not born a logical person, and there were times early on in my life where my thought processes were anything but, which was why I made a concerted effort after my mother died to always think through the logical routes before jumping to conclusions. To always see what is actually in front of me, rather than imagining and building scenarios in my head. Logic has not been an easy thing to learn. Therapy helped a lot. Holding myself accountable helps too. Now, logic is always my first port of call. That's why I have to tell myself I'm safe when my panic attacks kick in. Because it's true. I always am safe. Logic first, feelings later. That's how I've spent the last decade moving forward.

But strange as it may sound, it was also a logical decision to become an artist. I had spent years losing myself in my art, and every piece of work honed my skills. I knew it was something that I could start on a small scale with limited costs, sell online, then upscale as opportunities arose – which they did.

Even though I was making money without a formal education, art college was the next logical step, because I knew I needed to have the name of an establishment behind me. It didn't matter how good my work was on its own; logic told me I would not reach the levels of success I wanted without that endorsement. The only place in recent years that my logic has been a little sketchy in is my relationship with Patrick. It was absolutely not logical to fall in love with a married man, but it was logical to ensure that he was feeling the same way before I even considered progressing into a relationship with him. This house, with space for a growing family, in an area of the country that never devalues, and with room to expand and improve, was a logical step. But me seeing danger the way I've been doing since I moved here is not logical, and I don't like it one bit.

For a moment, I keep my eyes locked on the person and try to work out what to do. Yet before I can decide on the best course of action, they turn around and start walking away.

'Wait! Wait!' My voice is a yell and several heads turn in my direction, but I ignore them all. 'Who are you? What are you doing? Are you following me?' Before I can make any choice, logical or not, my legs are moving. Chasing after them. 'Wait!'

My pulse races as I follow them around the corner, into a wide alley where several people are clustered together, and none of them look like the person who was staring at me only a minute ago. 'Sorry! Sorry!' I say as I push past them, yet as I make my way through them, I stop. The alley opens up onto the junction of a road. The person could have gone in any direction. I've lost them.

With my breaths laboured and fast, I drop my hands onto my knees.

'What the hell are you doing, Imogen?' I say to myself. It's not a question I have an answer to right now. As I stand there, unsure where to go or what to do, my stomach growls. Other than the coffee we had before we went into the outbuilding, I've not eaten or drunk anything today. I never think particularly clearly when I haven't eaten, so there's my next logical step. Food. That's something I can do.

There are dozens of cafés that I can see down the high street, and I'm sure some have got far better reviews than others, but I'm not bothered about the standard of the food. What I want is somewhere I can sit quietly and get my head together. As such, I decide to skip the first place I walk past. The inside is absolutely rammed, and by the looks of things, there's a queue of people waiting for tables, too. That's normally the type of place I would want to go to – just to find out what all the fuss is about – but right now, I want quiet, so I keep walking until a bakery appears at the end of the road.

The large chain establishment looks pretty out of place in comparison to all the independent stores here, but it's near enough empty, and it sells coffee and food. Those are my only two requirements. I head to the counter, order my drink and a sandwich, then sit down.

'Let's think about this logically,' I say to myself as I take the lid off the coffee so it can cool down faster. The quicker it cools, the quicker I can get caffeine in my body. That's probably not the most logical decision given that my heart rate is already elevated, but it's what I need. A couple of sips in and my mind slows enough for me to think more clearly.

I was obviously shaken up after the car nearly ran me off the road. I'm almost 100 per cent sure it was an accident. An accident caused by an arsehole behind the wheel. After all, a decent person would have definitely stopped to make sure I was okay. But an accident, still. And as for the person standing on the corner of a building looking in my direction, well, everyone's got to look in some direction, don't they? Either that or you just stare at the ground or sky the entire time – and that would just be downright weird. So both those incidents I can pass off as accidents or insignificant. But as for the person standing up looking through the window last night... Even though what Patrick said made sense, my mind can't help but think there's something more to it. And that's what unnerves me. I'm not accepting his logic and I know how easy it can be to start spiralling. I know what it's like when one minute you think you've got a grip on things, and then, before you can even blink, it feels like the entire world is spinning and you have no way of knowing which way you're going to fall. All you know is that when you finally hit the ground, it's going to hurt like hell. I can't do that. I can't spiral when I'm planning on bringing a baby into the world. I promised myself I wouldn't. That I wouldn't put my child through the roller coaster I went through with my mother. It's not fair, which means I need to get a grip on things fast.

My sandwich is still sitting untouched in front of me, but rather than taking a bite, I pull out my phone and open a search page.

Can pregnancy cause anxiety?

The second I hit enter, the screen fills.

The hormone changes that occur during pregnancy result in as many as 30 per cent of women suffering from anxiety. Such symptoms include trouble sleeping, shaking, trembling or sweating, lack of focus, excessive worrying about baby's and mother's health, financial concerns...

The list goes on and on and there's no doubt I'm hitting a lot of the criteria. Way more that would happen if it was just a coincidence. So does that mean I'm pregnant? It sure as hell feels like it.

A feeling of excitement flutters within me, though as I pick up my sandwich, I wince. The scratches on my arm are no longer bleeding, but they're red and angry and probably need a good clean. There's a pharmacy down by the first coffee shop where I can pick up some antiseptic wipes before the ride back, and while I'm there, I might as well pick up a pregnancy test at the same time.

19

The clinic that we did the IVF through gave us a bunch of tests, but they're somewhere in the mix with all our boxes, and ignorantly I assumed it would be easier just to pick up a couple here now. Turns out I was wrong.

I imagine there was a time when, if you wanted a pregnancy test, you would go into a store and pick up the one type they had. But as I stand here, looking at the shelves, I'm suddenly overwhelmed by the choices in front of me. There are pregnancy strips, digital pregnancy tests, rapid detection tests and others which actually tell you how many weeks pregnant you are. There are even saliva pregnancy tests. I really didn't know saliva pregnancy tests were a thing.

It's definitely the early detection I need, so my hand reaches out to pick up that packet, but before I can, a woman sidles up beside me.

'Congratulations,' she says. 'It is congratulations, yes? Not an oopsie-daisy.'

I don't respond. I can't. I'm absolutely stunned to my core that a woman would think it's okay to come up to a complete stranger and say something like that. And she is a woman, not a girl. At a guess, she looks about thirty and has a few strands of grey glittering her mostly dark hair. Certainly old enough to know better. But before I can reply, she carries on.

'I know I shouldn't be nosy,' she says. 'It's one of my worst traits. It's just... it always makes me feel really happy, you know? Whenever I know there's a new baby being born in the world. You can't not be happy when there's a baby being born, can you?'

My mind flicks to my own childhood. Not just the way I was raised, but the way the children around me were raised, too. Kids who were truant for half of school for no other reason than because their parents didn't give enough of a shit to check up on them. Who were left to fend for themselves at an age where they should have had someone tucking them in and reading to them in bed each night. I think of that baby who was taken into care after I rang for help. If people had been happy when they were born, I can't imagine it ever would have reached that stage.

While the woman's gaze remains on me, awaiting an answer, I shift uncomfortably, unsure how to ask her to leave me alone and not randomly start talking to people buying pregnancy tests again. Yet before I can say anything, her cheeks flush a deep red.

'I'm sorry, I'm sorry. I'm not very good at knowing boundaries. It's one of my problems. That's why I'm here. I'm here picking these up.' She lifts her hands to show a brown paper bag with a white pharmacy label stuck on it. 'I should probably take one now,' she says, opening it up and pulling out a white box. The name is written in large pink writing on the front.

My stomach plummets. Is this some kind of joke?

She opens the packet and pops one of the pills into her mouth and swallows it without so much as a sip of water.

Although that's not what has caused my hands to tremble. I used to take tablets without water myself.

Those exact tablets. Those antipsychotic tablets.

As I stare at the package, my mind rushes back to all those years ago. To the days when the smell of death and decay filled our small flat and yet I carried on like everything was perfectly normal. To the days when the doctors wondered if I would ever recover from what I had been through.

That thought alone is enough to bring me back to the present. I did recover. I did the work, and that's why I'm in the position I'm in now. Successful, married to a man who loves me, and quite possibly having a baby with him. Without a glance at the woman, I snatch up the early detection pregnancy test and march away, only to stop when I reach the end of the aisle.

I need to say something. To tell her that what she just did was wildly inappropriate and that if she doesn't leave this instant, I will be telling security. Yet as I turn back to her, the words on the tip of my tongue, I find the aisle is empty.

She has already gone.

20

Twenty minutes later, my stomach is full, my arm is wiped clean and has been wrapped in a large dressing by the woman in the pharmacy, and there is a multipack of early detection pregnancy tests in my bag. The image of the woman, holding those tablets so casually in front of me, causes more than one shudder to roll down my spine, but I do my best to push her from my mind. She was harmless. Lonely, probably. That's why she was trying to start conversations with random people. Definitely not worth another moment's thought. Just like those tablets. My days of needing medication to know the difference between reality and what's going on in my head are long gone. After all, that one episode I had only lasted a couple of days. And considering the trauma I went through, it was hardly surprising. A couple of days' insanity compared to years and years of straight-headed thinking. There's no way I'm going to let those memories impact the life I've made for myself with Patrick. Not a chance.

On the way back to the bike, I pop into a little deli and admire the rows of pastrami, cured meats, and soft cheeses that have me practically drooling from the aromas. I don't know all the pregnancy rules yet, but I'm pretty sure those are off-limits. Although that doesn't mean Patrick can't eat them. I grab a few of his favourites and a couple of other things for me. Like vine leaves and olives and – in case the test is positive – a bottle of non-alcoholic bubbles, which probably tastes foul, but I doubt I'll care.

As I unclip the lock on the bike, my thoughts shift to Patrick. I know he's on a long journey to get rid of those awful taxidermy animals, but I should probably keep him updated on where I am, so he doesn't worry. I quickly fire off a message telling him I'm leaving town now, then hop on the bike and start heading back.

I know so much in life is a case of mind over matter, but sometimes the mind is a pain in the backside and after fifteen minutes into the journey back, I realise the accident has shaken me more than I first thought. I'm riding unusually slowly and my legs feel heavy and sluggish as I push the pedals. Can pregnancy affect your ability to cycle? Obviously, when you've got a bump, that's going to affect how you balance, but can the hormones throw it off too? My muscles ache like I'm working on top resistance in a spin class, yet my pace is getting slower and slower. With my breaths heaving, I give it a bit more effort, trying to pick up speed, but instead of moving faster, the bike seems to struggle.

I'm just under halfway home when it hits me – maybe *I'm* not the problem. Maybe it's the bike.

I glance down at the back wheel and, sure enough, it's completely flat.

'You have got to be kidding me,' I mutter, climbing off the bike to inspect it more closely.

There is no way I can ride it like this. It's a miracle I even got this far. Drawing in a long breath, I try to work out what to do.

There's a puncture repair kit in my bag, but no pump. I always thought that I'd notice before a tyre got this flat. Apparently not. Besides, cycling in London is different. There were always dozens of other cyclists around who would have been able to help me out had this happened. But here, I've not seen another bike since I left the town. I flick the wheel with my hand, spinning it around to see if there's any sign of what caused the hole. My first thought is that it must've been a bramble from when I crashed into the hedge earlier. A thorn could've punctured the rubber and I wouldn't have noticed if the air was leaking out slow enough.

But as I spin the wheel, something glints in the sunlight.

I move the tyre around until I'm looking at that exact spot, and a hollowness sweeps through me.

This puncture wasn't a bramble, and it wasn't an accident either.

21

I don't think about the fact I'm standing on the edge of a narrow road or how, only a couple of hours ago, I feared for my life on a road just like this. I don't look around to see if there's room for cars to pass, or step further onto the verge. Instead, I remain exactly where I am, unable to take my eyes off those drawing pins. Three of them, placed horizontally across the width of the tyre, touching ever so slightly, perfectly aligned.

This was no accident. There's no way I could have ridden over something so precisely placed and not noticed. Someone did this. Someone *wanted* this to happen to me. My mind flicks to the woman in the pharmacy. Could she have done this? Could she have seen me as some type of threat, and if that's the case, what else might she do?

My temperature plummets momentarily only for a heat to rise in my chest, threatening to engulf me in panic, but I can't lose it here. Not on the side of the road. I have to hold myself together. I need to get home.

I drop my backpack and grab my phone, knowing full well that the reception here is terrible. Still, I have to try. A wave of disappointment hits when I see, once again, that there are zero bars. The screen clearly says 'emergency calls only'. This *is* an emergency – someone tampered with my bike. But I know that's not the kind of emergency they mean. I can't waste police time with something like this.

I don't have a choice. I just have to keep going.

Walking should be easy – it normally is. I can walk for hours without breaking a sweat. Cycling, too, is normally effortless. But pushing a bike with a flat tyre is a whole different story. I feel every bump. Every turn requires my muscles to pull and push on the handlebars, and every pothole that seemed insignificant on my ride here now makes this trek a thousand times harder. And while the day itself is cool, I am anything but.

When I was cycling, the combination of exercise and the breeze kept me comfortable, but now, even after shedding my jacket and slinging my helmet over the handlebars, sweat drips down my back. Every step feels like a battle. When I reach the turning for our lane, I want to cry in relief, although as Maureen's cottage appears, I find myself holding my breath. The last thing I can deal with right now is her coming out with that giant dog of hers and disclosing yet more horror stories about our new home. Although thankfully, there's no sign of her.

There is, however, another car. One I recognise instantly. I drop the bike against the gate and run to the driver's door, before swinging it open without a second's thought.

'What are you doing here?' I say. 'Why didn't you tell me you were coming?'

22

Orla's face beams as she slips out of the car and wraps her arms around me.

My agent is one of those women you never see smile in public. She's all business, and I know it can put some people off her. Particularly given her very public-school, very Queen's English accent. Just her saying hello can sound like she's looking down on you. But I've known her far too long for that. Like Brutus, Orla is definitely a case of her bark being worse than her bite. Not that I'd like to risk it with Brutus.

'I wanted to surprise you,' she said. 'Plus, I wasn't sure I'd be down this way so soon, but then I got a phone call first thing this morning about an exhibition space to check out – so I thought I'd drop in. To be honest, I was sure you were out. I was only going to hang around another ten minutes before heading off.'

'I'm so glad you stayed. Come in, let me give you a tour. If you have time, that is?'

'Absolutely.'

'Great, although there's not much to tour at the minute –

we've got the furniture in and everything, but we want to change a lot.'

'It's a lovely light space,' Orla says as she walks in. 'So much potential. I can't wait to see what it'll be like when you're done. You can get the girls down. Have a proper housewarming party.'

I feel a flash of guilt as she says this. The girls she's referring to are the group of friends from art college. For several years we were inseparable, and even now, we make sure we go to every event or exhibition one of us has, but between work and Patrick and IVF, it's got harder and harder to find time to see them. I guess that's not going to get any easier if I'm pregnant, and so I make a mental note to put a date in the diary for us to get together. One that's less than nine months from now.

'Well, there's a long way to go yet,' I say, my mind returning back to the conversation.

'You'll get there. No doubt you'll turn the place into a work of art.'

All the stresses of the day feel as though they're melting away as I head into the kitchen and flick on the kettle. There's no point checking she actually wants a drink; Orla is one of those people that drinks tea from the moment she wakes up until the moment she goes to bed, only stopping for her two daily coffees. She's always been that way. I met her in college. She was in the year below me and incredibly talented. Not to mention focused. But as gifted an artist as she is, she was even more gifted as a salesperson. She fell into the agent role naturally, and she's the only agent I've ever worked with – the only one I'd ever want to work with. She's a friend first, and I like it that way. It means I can be open and honest when I don't like some ideas. Of course, that's not without its occasional issues.

'I'm so sorry about that interview the other day,' she says, taking off her coat. 'They're going to send me the piece, and I'll fire it across to you as soon as I've got it. I'm sure it'll be brilliant, though. They know better than to pry. Everyone knows better than to pry.'

By everyone, I feel like she's talking about herself too. Orla knows bits and pieces about my past. Definitely more than most people. She knows I went off the rails when my mother died, and I think she assumes it means the usual – drinking, drugs, maybe some wild behaviour. She couldn't be more wrong, but that's okay. I'm happy to let her think whatever she needs to.

'So, where's the studio?' she asks as I hand her her tea. 'I can't wait to see where the magic happens.'

'Well, there's no magic happening at the minute. It was full of taxidermy animals this morning.'

Her eyes widen. 'You're joking! Seriously?'

'I wish I was. I went out for a bike ride and let Patrick deal with it. He's driven up to Oxford to give them away to someone.'

Her expression of horror remains fixed as she takes a sip of her drink, but as she pulls the mug away from her lips, a smile is twisted tightly on them. 'Right, well, I still want to see the space. Maybe I can help you sort it out. I've got a couple of hours before I need to head off.'

'You don't want to spend your spare time helping me clean up my studio.'

'Sure I do. I helped set up your last one, remember? It'll be like reliving the good old days.'

'I'm not sure I'd consider being a near-penniless artist as the good old days,' I say. 'But if you really don't mind, some help would be great.'

23

'Wow, this is an amazing space.' Orla's jaw hangs loose as she takes it all in. 'I mean, it has so much potential. And it's all set up with heating and lights, right? And the sink? What a bonus.'

'I know. We didn't even see inside the place until this morning,' I admit. 'We could estimate the size, and I knew it'd be light from all the windows, but still...'

'I can't wait to see what you create in here,' she says, stepping further into the studio, though as she moves forward, her phone starts ringing. 'Sorry, just a second,' she says, smiling apologetically. 'I need to get this.' A moment later, she steps out to take the call, leaving me alone in my studio for the first time.

At least half of the boxes are gone, and the rest have been opened. Just a glance tells me the ones that are left all contain craft supplies, tools, wires, that type of thing. Patrick must've gone through them all to check for the taxidermy creatures.

If someone had asked me to list qualities of a perfect partner, removing dead animals from my home wouldn't have made the list. But right now, I'm so glad he did it.

With the extra space cleared, I can see just how much room

the building has. It's going to need a good clean-up, but it's already usable. The shelves, though rusted in some places, look sturdy enough to hold my paints and supplies, and as I turn on the tap, there's a gurgle and glug of brown water, but it takes only a few moments to clear.

I'm still rinsing out the sink when Orla reappears.

'Okay, so my afternoon plans have been cancelled,' she says. 'Which means we have even more time to get this space in order. I reckon by the time I leave, this studio is going to be ready to work in.'

'Are you sure you don't mind?' I say. 'You could drive back to London now and miss the rush-hour traffic.'

She shrugs. 'I think it'll do me some good to be here. You know, maybe give me some inspiration and motivation to do an exhibition of my own.'

Despite all her contacts, Orla rarely shows her work any more, although she occasionally takes the odd commission. I'm sure she's got a thousand more useful ways she could spend her afternoon than be here with me, but I've given her plenty of get outs and I'm not going to turn down the help again.

'Okay then,' I say. 'Time to get cleaning. And just so you know, you're dealing with any dead mice or rats. Spiders I can do, but that's it.'

'That's not a deal I'm willing to make,' she says, laughing.

As Orla rolls up her sleeves, I head back into the kitchen, where I fill a bowl with warm, soapy water, grab a cloth, and then return to the outbuilding.

While Orla remains inside the studio, I start on the outside of the windows, but I quickly regret using a damp cloth; one wipe in and it's clogged with cobwebs and grime. Dropping it into the bowl, I switch tactics and grab a brush from the dustpan to knock off the big cobwebs before wiping down the glass. It's a long job and I lose count of how many times I go into the house for clean warm water, but as soon as I step back into the studio, I realise how much of a difference it's made already.

'It's looking good,' Orla says. 'I've cleared out the sink and wiped down most of the shelves, and I was about to make a start on the windows, but we're going to have to move these boxes first. A couple of them are pretty heavy. Can you give me a hand?'

I try to keep my expression steady. I might not know the ins and outs of what foods you're allowed when you're pregnant, but I know you're not meant to lift things. And while Orla knows that we were trying IVF, I'm not sure sharing the news about the implantation with *her* is something I'm up to doing. After all, if it hasn't worked, that means I'd have to tell her that too.

'Why don't we try pushing them,' I say. 'My back's not been great recently.'

'Nothing serious, is it?'

I shake my head, annoyed at myself for adding a lie that I'm now going to have to expand on. 'No, it's all fine,' I say. 'I think I was just overdoing it yesterday travelling, moving boxes.'

'Okay, well, I'm sure we can figure it out. Maybe if you can just help balance them?'

The saying 'many hands make light work' has never felt truer. Orla is a workhorse, and I've always known that, but after two hours, we've stopped moving things from the studio and are finally moving in my supplies.

'Where do you want your dryers, and why do you have so many?' she asks, pulling out four from a box. One is a regular hairdryer, but the others are designed for different types of paint. You can get great effects by drying paints at different speeds. 'I didn't know addiction to hairdryers was a thing.'

'Not an addiction,' I say, laughing. 'I just need them.'

'Fine,' she says with mock exasperation. 'I'll put them on the shelf up here. Is that okay?'

'Yeah, no problem.'

As she finishes arranging my dryers, she turns to look at me.

'I think it's time we stop for a cup of tea. What do you say? Are you okay to stop for now?'

I lock my eyes straight on hers. 'Honestly, I thought you'd never ask,' I say with a laugh.

24

Orla sits at the kitchen table with her second mug of tea in her hand, although unusually she's barely taken a sip of it. Instead, she keeps glancing at her phone and pursing her lips.

'Is everything all right?' I say. 'You really don't have to stay. If you need to go, I don't mind. Just seeing you has been a surprise I wasn't expecting.'

'Yeah, I know. About that.' Her lips purse again, this time with so much force that her cheeks draw inwards. 'I need to be honest with you, Im. I lied about why I turned up here. I don't have another meeting. I needed to come and see you.'

'Really? You could've just said that.' For a second, I think she's alluding to the closeness of our friendship, but if that's the case, why does she look so nervous? My stomach drops. Friendship isn't why she's here at all.

'Orla?'

She bites down on her bottom lip as she grips the mug.

'Look, you know I love this work that you've been doing. I really do. But it's not going to sell. None of the old galleries I've spoken to are interested. They've already got a dozen artists doing the same thing. They don't think there's a market for it.'

I shake my head. 'That doesn't make any sense. If they already have artists with a similar style, then there has to be a market. Besides, I am Imogen Cromford, for crying out loud. They should be falling over themselves to get to me.' I sound like an arrogant prick, I know, but I've spent a long time building up my name. To be told it's worthless, by the person who's supposed to be my biggest cheerleader, is a damn big blow.

'I know what you're saying. I do.' Orla's hands have left her mug and are open and facing me, as if she's trying to block my words. 'But the name Imogen Cromford evokes a feeling. Tension. Darkness. Uncertainty. People can see all the torment in your work. It's a comfort, knowing someone else has felt that pain too. That's what they want. Not your current style.'

I look at her, my chest tightening. 'So, what do you want me to do? Are you saying I need to go back to what I was doing before? I won't do that. You know how much it took out of me.'

'I do, I understand that.'

She doesn't. She says she does, but she can't. No one could. The memories I drew on each time I picked up a paintbrush to create one of those 'tormented' pieces, as she likes to call them, nearly broke me. The famous 'Cromford Blue' isn't just a colour I took a fancy to. It's a shade that's seared into my memory. One I won't ever be able to forget, even if I wanted to. But that doesn't mean I have to put myself through the agony of painting with it every day.

'I won't do it, Orla,' I say.

'I was worried that would be your response, Im. Look, just take some time. It's not like you need the money right now.'

At the mention of my finances, I feel my jaw dropping.

'Why did you come here, Orla? What is it you actually came to say?'

She draws in a lungful of air, and I watch her chest expand before she lets it out with a sigh. 'Imogen... this isn't easy for me, either. I want you to know that. But I don't think this direction you're heading in is best suited to having me as your agent. I'm sorry.'

'You're dropping me as a client because I've got... happy?' I choke out. 'Because I couldn't live my entire life using my mental health to make other people happy?'

'You know that's not what it is. But you need the right advocate for your work. Someone who can scream from the rooftops about how wonderful it is. If you could just try to paint some of the darker things again. Rework some of your old pieces?'

She looks at me, her eyes pleading, but my silence says all it needs to.

'Thank you for coming round,' I say eventually, standing up as I speak. 'And for your help with the studio. Do you remember where the front door is?'

25

‘Hey, why haven’t you got the lights on?’ Patrick says when he comes in and kisses me on the forearm. ‘Is everything all right? How was your bike ride? How’s your arm? I’m so sorry I wasn’t here.’

‘Fuck, the bike,’ I say, almost surprised at how quickly I’ve forgotten about it. ‘Today has proven that the saying “bad things come in threes” is bullshit.’

‘Really, what happened?’ He drops into the seat beside me. ‘Not Maureen?’

‘No,’ I say, shaking my head. ‘I’ve not seen her. Thank God.’ I try to figure out the best place to begin, not that there is a good place when everything you have to say is negative. Still, I start with Orla. Since she left, my disbelief has shifted to anger and then outright fury.

‘At least she didn’t drop you by a phone call?’ he says, trying to sound optimistic. It doesn’t work.

‘She was here for hours, helping me sort out my studio, like she actually gave a damn about my work. I’d have rather had a phone call than that type of manipulation.’

Patrick's nostrils flare as he breathes in, yet when he exhales, he somehow turns the expression into a smile.

'You know what? This could be a good thing.'

'Really?'

'Yeah, she's been taking her cut for doing nothing for years now. Maybe she helped you make a name for yourself, but when was that – ten years ago? And to be honest, I think you could have done it without her. No, this is good. You can go back to selling direct, online. You've got so many long-term collectors that will continue to buy your work. It'll be amazing. And they'll actually support this journey you're on. Trust me, this is going to work out well. I can feel it.'

Hearing him speak like that gives me my first hint of calm and relief. He's right, of course. I can sell online. It shouldn't take too long to build up a social media following, given the name I've already got for myself.

'So, what about the rest of the day? Was the bike ride back any better?'

Instantly, all the tension returns to my muscles. The cold fear I felt at seeing the person on the corner watching me causes my arms to rise in goosebumps. Once again, my ability to be logical is slipping.

'I know what you said last night about the stress and everything, but today I've felt like someone is targeting me.'

'What?' His jaw drops so fast I swear I hear a click. 'What do you mean? Is this about the car that nearly hit you? I thought you said it was an accident, that they didn't see you.'

'I thought that too. But then I swear there was someone watching me, and there was this really strange incident in the pharmacy with this woman and then, on the ride back, there were pins stuck in the tyre.'

His brow furrows. 'Pins? What kind of pins?'

'Drawing pins. Three of them stuck into the rim in a perfectly straight line. I'll show you. It wasn't an accident. It can't have been.'

His jaw hangs open now, though he's no longer speaking. He blinks as he processes what I've said.

'So what happened? How did you get back? Did you dump the bike and walk?'

Hearing him say that makes me realise what an obvious solution that would have been. I could've left it, walked back in almost half the time, then driven back with the car to pick it up. It's just a sign of how muddled my mind must have been that the thought didn't even cross it.

'I wheeled it back.'

'With a flat tyre? That must have taken you forever.'

'Yeah, it did. But that can't be an accident, can it? Three drawing pins, in a perfectly straight line.'

'It does sound weird,' he admits. 'But…'

'But?' I press when he lets his sentence fade to nothing.

He reaches across and takes my hand. 'You know, heightened anxiety can be a symptom of pregnancy,' he tells me. 'I'm not saying that it didn't happen, but do you think that maybe your reaction could be something to do with that?' His lips twitch as if he wants to smile but isn't sure he should.

'I thought that too.' My own lips want to rise, but I keep them in place. Yet it's harder to do when Patrick takes my hands.

'So, do you think you might be?'

'I bought a test. Well, several tests, actually.'

I still want to get to the bottom of those damn drawing pins, but maybe this isn't the time. Not with the way Patrick is beaming at me.

'Oh my God!' he says. 'Really? This is amazing! This is the best news. This is… Shit.'

'This is shit?' I say, confused by the sudden turn.

'No! No, sorry, this is definitely not shit.' He shakes his head and laughs. 'Not at all. Only I know I was going to take the entire week off to help us settle into the house, but James rang while I was driving, and it seems like they're all stressing about the merger and I was going to see if you were okay with me going in, but now I really don't want to. Not with the chance that I'll be leaving two of you here alone.'

A flutter of relief escapes my lungs. Patrick is a workaholic. He was like that when I met him. It was one of the reasons Arabella never suspected he was having an affair – of course, back then, he *was* spending a lot of time at the office just to get a bit of freedom from her. Still, his addiction to work didn't change when we got married, and I didn't expect it to change now that we've moved here. After all, there was a reason we had to look for somewhere within easy driving distance from a train station.

'It's fine, of course it's fine,' I say. 'I'm surprised you managed these two days. I thought you'd be back at work today.'

'You did not,' he says.

'Oh, I absolutely did.' I grin, fighting the urge to kiss him.

'Well, I was thinking I could get the early train, stay the night, and then come back on Thursday evening. That way, I wouldn't have to go in on Friday, and we could have a three-day weekend. How does that sound?'

'That sounds great,' I say, trying to ignore the churning in my stomach. It's just anxiety, I remind myself. Hormones because I might be pregnant. I'll be fine. I'm sure I'll be fine.

26

Our picky dinner goes well. Patrick doesn't say much about the man he delivered the taxidermy to.

'He was odd,' he says, spearing a piece of cheese. 'Odd and old. He invited me in, but I made the excuse of having the long drive back. How was the town? Somewhere you think you might be able to draw some inspiration?'

'Definitely,' I say. But that's never been an issue for me – my mind's constantly overflowing with ideas. It's not about finding inspiration; it's about calming my mind enough to sit and bring an idea to life.

'Did you pass through any of the little villages at all? Speak to anyone?'

'No,' I say, shaking my head. 'I mean, I rode through a village or two, but I didn't see anyone to speak to. I guess most people are at work.'

'Right? It might be useful to go online. You know, see if there are any mum and baby groups that meet locally. Sign the little one up for baby gymnastics. That type of thing.'

'I think it'll be a fair while until we have to worry about

things like that,' I reply, although annoyingly my mind lingers on the word 'worry'. The thought of there not being enough for our children to do automatically makes me think of how the kids up at Springfield Farm dealt with their boredom. Should we worry about raising our children here? Do we really want them to grow up in a place where boredom might tempt them into trouble? Would we have been better off staying in London, where they'd have drama groups, sports teams, and endless things to do? But then again, it'll be at least a decade before we have to worry about any of that.

'Are you okay?' Patrick asks, placing his hand over mine. 'You look a little distracted.'

'I'm fine,' I say, shaking myself out of the moment. 'I think the cycle ride wore me out more than I expected.'

'I suspect it was pushing the bike that did it,' he says, 'but you're right, you need to rest. Why don't you go upstairs, have a bath, get into bed, and read? I'll clean up here and join you in a bit.'

'Sure, that sounds good.'

We've got two bathrooms in the house: the main one, which has both a bath and a shower, and an ensuite with just a shower. The main bathroom needs redecorating for aesthetics, but the bath is good, even if the shower pressure is terrible. I head in and turn on the hot water tap, yet as the tub fills and the steam starts to build, I change my mind and turn it off.

In one of our IVF sessions, the nurse mentioned something about avoiding overly hot baths. I'm the type who likes the water so hot that by the time I get out, my skin is red. Right now, that doesn't feel like the type of thing I should do. And a cool bath is a substantially less appealing option. Abandoning the idea of a long soak, I decide to shower in the ensuite instead.

As I move back into the bedroom, I hear Patrick talking on the phone.

'You need to trust me about this.'

There's an urgency in his voice, an edge of weariness. I assume he's talking to someone from work, maybe someone who isn't keen on following instructions. I've always loved listening to Patrick when he's in work mode – so professional, so skilled. It's a huge turn-on. I move to the top of the stairs, tingles spreading through me as I think how far I've come from that tower block apartment. Here I am now, living in a beautiful house with a man like Patrick. Sometimes I have to pinch myself.

'You know that I do,' he says, his voice clearer now. 'Of course I love you. Nothing will ever change that.'

My heart skips a beat. Unable to stop myself, I move another step closer.

'What the hell…' I murmur just before he speaks again.

'I'll always love you.'

27

I feel sick. My head spins as I struggle to keep my balance. Stumbling back, I grab the banister for support. Patrick is on the phone, in *our* new house, telling someone else that he loves them. What the hell?

A wave of nausea rolls through me. I can't believe it. I *refuse* to believe it. Patrick can't be cheating on me. After everything he went through with Arabella, there's no way he'd do that to me. Would he? My mind races. All the things he said about the tension in their house affecting Prim... how that was why they sent her to boarding school...

Prim.

The realisation hits me like a gasp of air. There's only one other person Patrick would say he loves, who he'd do anything for.

'Fucking hormones,' I mutter, gritting my teeth. I never expected it to be like this. It's one thing struggling to keep my thoughts straight, but this... jumping to conclusions and thinking Patrick is having an affair. Why would I do that? I trust him explicitly. My mind flickers to the multiple tests I bought.

Do I really want to risk taking one early? A false negative or false positive would hurt. A lot. I'd much rather wait until I've got an accurate answer.

Content that Patrick isn't cheating on me, and that I've got enough patience to wait another two days to take the test, I head to the shower. My arm stings as I examine the cuts and scratches. I was lucky – I can see that now. But rather than feeling relief, I'm *angry*. That car could have seriously hurt me, but what if it hadn't been me on the road? What if it had been a teenager? Or an older person; someone who didn't grow up wearing helmets and still refuses to believe they were unsafe on quiet country lanes? What if I hadn't landed in a bramble bush, but had been thrown into a tree, or a lamppost?

The what ifs roll around in my mind. I wanted to let it go, I really did, but now I'm not so sure. Maybe I'll ask Maureen if she knows anyone locally who drives a green four-by-four. I'm sure she won't miss out on the chance for a bit of gossip.

By the time Patrick comes up to bed, I'm feeling strangely calm. As annoyed as I was – *am* – at Orla, she did help me clear out the studio, meaning I can start working on whatever I want. Maybe a new collection inspired by this place. Patrick being gone will also give me a chance to get the house straight. Maybe order some new curtains or pieces of furniture.

'I thought you'd be asleep by now,' he says as he steps into the bedroom. 'You looked exhausted at dinner.'

'I know, but I've just been thinking lots. And reading.' I sink into the pillow, dropping my book on the nightstand.

'So, how's Prim?'

'Prim? She texted me yesterday, wishing us luck for the move. But I haven't heard from her today. I think I might meet up with her for lunch tomorrow, when I'm in town. If she's free of course. You know what her social calendar is like.'

'Did you not speak to her just now?' I say, my stomach twisting. 'I thought I heard you on the phone.'

'The phone?' He frowns, before shaking his head and laughing. 'Oh, yes. Sorry, you're right. It was just a quick check in, that's all.'

Without another word he turns away from me and switches the light off. Almost like he doesn't want me to see his face. Like if I can see his expression, I'll be able to tell that he's lying to me, but it's too late for that. The knowledge hits me like a hammer to the chest. Patrick is having an affair.

28

I love you. That's what he said. *I'll always love you.* I'm sure of it. Patrick told someone he loved them while he was on the phone. Who the hell was he speaking to if it wasn't Prim? Unless he was, and he did genuinely forget, but that's not something he would do. Just like Prim wouldn't have wished us luck for the move. She wants my entire life to be a failure, particularly my marriage to her father. But who else could he have been talking to? I'm not even sure I want to know.

Sleep refuses to come. I toss and turn, unable to find a temperature that my body likes, let alone make my mind settle. Every time I start to drift off, a thought jerks me awake. Patrick's voice. The pins in the tyre. The figure outside the window. Then the scratching starts again. So much for thinking I could live with it. I am calling an exterminator this week and getting rid of whatever is in there. Then again, maybe it's not worth it. If Patrick really is cheating on me, there's no point staying here. Maybe I'll pack up and move properly this time. I could go to Europe. Or even further. At least Prim would be happy.

Around 3 a.m., I give up, go downstairs, and grab a glass of water. Other than the vermin in the attic, the house is eerily quiet. It's never quiet in London, no matter what time it is. There's always the sound of traffic, people coming home from late shifts, or leaving for early ones. Babies crying, couples fighting. Even in the nicest parts of the city, silence doesn't exist. But here, it does. Here, I can hear every creak of the floorboards and Patrick's soft snore, which usually doesn't bother me but right now feels like a full-on growl as it echoes through the walls.

As I sip at the drink, my thoughts try to shift to logic. Could this be part of the pregnancy paranoia I read about while sitting in the café? I know how powerful the mind is. How it can make you believe or even see things that aren't there. It's part of a protection mechanism. That's what it was before. But why would thinking Patrick was cheating on me protect me? Maybe because I'm worried about him hurting me? No. I'm not worried about that. Maybe at the beginning of the relationship, but he broke up his family for us. Why would he have gone through IVF with me if he wasn't serious? Why would he have looked so happy at the news that I might be pregnant? As the thoughts flitter through my mind, my eyes fall on a small rectangular object charging on the kitchen counter – Patrick's phone. There's one way to know if it was all in my head or not, and that would be to look at his recently called list.

The way my hands are trembling is a sign that I know I shouldn't do what I'm about to. It's an invasion of privacy. A lack of trust. He's my husband. If I trusted him enough to marry him, I should trust that he was telling me the truth about his phone call, shouldn't I? But either Patrick is lying to me or I'm going insane, and right now I'm not sure which I'd prefer to be true. With a deep breath, I reach out, grab the phone, and type in the passcode.

It doesn't work.

'What?' I know Patrick's passcode. It's our wedding anniversary, the same code as mine. Why would he have changed it? With my hands trembling so much it's hard to press the right keys, I try again. This time, the phone unlocks. So I was the problem, not a changed passcode. And now I'm in.

'Do you really want to do this, Imogen?' I whisper aloud. Maybe if the password hadn't worked again, if he'd changed his passcode, I would've taken it as a sign that he was trying to conceal something from me, but the fact I can still get into it is surely a sign that he's got nothing to hide.

As much as I want to put the phone down, I've already come too far. I can't go to bed without checking. I just can't. Before I can stop myself, I tap the phone symbol at the bottom of the screen while simultaneously squeezing my eyes shut. Whatever I see now might change my life in ways I'm not ready for. After all, there's a good chance Patrick's child is growing inside me. If I trust him enough to have his baby, surely I should trust him enough to let this go?

I don't want to do this, but I have to.

With a sharp breath in, I open my eyes and look at the screen.

29

Numbness – that's the feeling flowing through me. If that can even be considered a feeling. Numbness and confusion. I feel my brow crease as I look at the screen in front of me. The perfectly blank screen. There's nothing on it at all. None of the calls from me earlier in the day. None of the work conversations that I'm sure would have taken place. Not even the number for the taxidermist that he spoke to earlier. The recent call list on Patrick's phone is completely blank. He's deleted it. He's deleted his call list, and it can only mean one thing.

He didn't want me to see it. I was right. Patrick told someone else on the phone that he loved them. He's cheating on me. *Patrick is cheating on me.*

'You fucking idiot, Imogen,' I say, wiping the tears from my eyes. As furious as I am at him, right now, my anger is directed inwards. What did I think was going to happen when I had an affair with a married man? What's that saying? Once a cheat, always a cheat? I guess as I was the other woman, I didn't want to believe it, but there's no point denying it now.

For a second, I sit there, wondering what my body is going to do. It feels like it might implode with all the pain coursing through it, yet I know it won't. There are none of the telltale panic attack signs either. Just a searing agony in my chest.

As I sit there, a hundred scenarios play out in my mind. I could confront him now, wake him up and tell him I know. Tell him I heard exactly what he said on the phone and that I know he deleted his call list. We could have it out here and now, and I could end it. But is that what I want? *Fuck!* What kind of woman has he made me that I don't even know what I want to do, even though I know he's cheating on me? I look at the phone screen again, praying that maybe it was a glitch and the calls have reappeared, but there's no such luck.

Ditch him. It's the only logical answer, and the voice in my head shouts it so loudly I want to take notice, but why is it that when it comes to Patrick, my brain throws logic to the curb?

I have been happier with him than I've ever been in my life. I've felt more secure, more confident. My art has been phenomenal, in my opinion at least. I've finally been able to move past the hold my mother and her death had on me. Patrick has made my entire life better, and I thought I'd done the same for him. But obviously, that wasn't the case.

How long has it been going on? That's the first question I want to ask him. *How long?* Long enough for him to tell her he loves her – that's one thing I know. And Patrick has always told me he isn't one to fall in love fast. He and Arabella grew up together; they were best friends going into secondary school and even then, it took years for him to admit his feelings.

I was the only person he had fallen for fast. The only one he had told he had said, 'I love you' to first – and within only a couple of months. But maybe that was just a line he spun me? *And why bother?* He'd already got me into bed. What would he gain? A man who wants to play around and chase women doesn't put a ring on the finger of the first woman he has an affair with. He sure as hell doesn't move to the other side of the country and plan to have a baby with her. If he'd been wanting to call things off, why wouldn't he have done it before now? He's not been distant, he's not been unloving. It doesn't make sense.

For the next hour, I snoop through his phone messages. His WhatsApp. His Facebook – which only has spam messages now. And there's nothing. No hint of any infidelity. Surely there should be some more evidence, shouldn't there? Something more than a deleted phone list.

I sit there at the kitchen table until I hear the first trill of the dawn chorus. Only then do I realise just how exhausted I am. I don't want to face him. I don't want to have to look at Patrick and tell him he's broken my heart, but with only the master bedroom made up I can either go up there or fall asleep on the sofa, and if I do that, he'll certainly wake me up before he goes to work. Then we'll have to have a conversation and that will be even more unbearable. With the decision made, I plug Patrick's phone back in and head upstairs.

30

I roll over in the bed, and for a second everything feels fine. Muted morning light seeps in through a gap in the curtain, and a shaft of light cuts across the room towards me. I feel incredibly at peace. And then I remember the phone.

The manner in which my stomach plummets is instant and so physical it's hard to believe it hasn't been caused by a physical stimulus. For a second, I struggle to remember the source of the feeling, and then I remember Patrick is having an affair. That's what I think has caused the reaction until I go to sit up. The nausea sweeps through me. I leap out of bed, dash towards the bathroom and, as my stomach contents lands in the toilet bowl, I realise there is likely more than one cause of this sickness.

There's nothing but bile in my stomach, but I empty it all. When I'm done, my throat is stinging and my eyes are watering. My gaze falls on the pregnancy tests next to the sink. One more day until I can take them, though it's feeling less and less likely that I need to. But rather than the excitement and optimism that I'd been feeling, it's uncertainty and fear that cloud me. I didn't want to be a single parent. It's the reason I'd never had a serious relationship before. I'd met guys that I liked and dated them for a few months, but I could never have seen them being the father of my children. I couldn't see them working with me as a team to raise them into adults. With Patrick, it was different. It didn't matter that he was older. Maybe that was actually what attracted me to him. He'd done it once before with Prim – and okay, he hadn't done the greatest job there, what with her being an entitled, manipulative bitch, but it wasn't all his fault. In fact, he was working away so much, most of the blame undoubtedly lay with Arabella. Besides, he knew that there were things he could do differently. Just like I knew there were things I would do very differently to how my mother did. We were going to go into parenthood with our eyes open, experience on his side. That's what I thought, anyway.

Now I can't be sure.

It's only when I go to get dressed that I find the note next to my pillow.

Have a great day. Love you.

P.S. there's a present in the studio for you.

Twenty-four hours ago, a note like that would have made my heart swell, but now it causes a ripple of tension to roll down my spine. Is he buying me off? Does he know I looked through his phone and this is just a way of trying to distract me? I dismiss the idea almost immediately. It's not like he could have bought something during the night. So maybe he got it earlier in the day when he was feeling guilty. That would make more sense.

As I stare at the note, I place my hands on my belly. I don't even know if that's the spot where the embryo will be, or how many embryos have even been successful, but I feel a connectedness. A sense of security. Even if what I fear about Patrick is true, then I'm not on my own. I'm not my mother. And I don't just mean in terms of the issues she had. I'm wealthy. My child will be able to go to a good school. They'll have neighbours with gardens, rather than neighbours with drug addictions. Even if I am on my own, and raising a child in a manner I hoped I'd never have to, it will not have the same upbringing as me.

With a newfound sense of strength, I head downstairs. I know there are all these rules about caffeine when you're pregnant, and Patrick brought me some fancy decaf for the French press, just so I didn't feel like I was missing out, but this morning I'm having the real thing. I'll make it weaker than normal. A half-shot latte maybe. That's what I think until I step into the kitchen.

'What the hell?'

31

I'm standing in the doorway, unable to move. Every cupboard and drawer in the kitchen is open. Every single one. The cupboard below the sink, the drawer above the oven. There's not a single one that remains closed. Even the fridge and freezer are open. What the hell is going on?

I rush over to the front door, half expecting to find it open, but it's not. The back door too is still locked closed. Panic surges through me. Why would someone do this? Who would do this? What the hell am I supposed to do? Ring Patrick, that's my first thought. So that's what I do.

He picks up my phone on the first ring.

'Hey, baby.' Patrick's voice is full of warmth. 'Did you like your present? I know it's a bit silly, but I just wanted to get you something to remind you how much I love you. That's all.'

'Did you do this?' I say, a hollow breathiness in my voice.

'Yeah, I left you a note. Did you not see it? It was on my pillow.'

I shake my head in frustration. 'I'm talking about the kitchen. The drawers – did you open them?'

'What? Did I leave something open? I just grabbed a coffee...'

My teeth grind together as my hands claw around my phone. Knowing this conversation will only go around in circles, I hang up the phone and then dial straight back, this time with a video call.

'This,' I say. 'Did you do this? Every cupboard is open. The knife drawer. The saucepan cupboard. Everything.'

I watch Patrick's eyes narrow as he scrutinises the picture he's seeing.

'I don't understand,' he says.

'I'm in the kitchen,' I say unnecessarily. 'I came down, and it was like this. Everything was open. Did you do this? Did you do this to me?'

'What? Of course I didn't! Have you checked the doors? The front and back doors? Are they both locked?'

'Yes, I've already done that,' I snap.

He's nodding his head. Biting down on his bottom lip as he nods his chin up and down.

'It looks like a prank,' he says finally. 'Maybe it's something the Springfield children would do. What about the windows? Did you see if any of the windows were open?'

The only window in the kitchen is directly above the sink, and that's closed, so there's no way they could have got in or out of there. With Patrick still on the call, I move through the rest of the house. I go into the dining room first, where both windows are closed. The living room is the same. The only other room is a small box room we were going to use as one of our offices. When I step in, I feel a flutter of cold air. The curtain ripples slightly.

'Here! Fuck!' I say as I move over to it.

'Have you found something?' Patrick says. I turn the camera

around to show him. One of the windows is a quarter of an inch ajar.

'They must have come in through this one,' I say, reaching out to close it, only to struggle. I tug it towards me, but it doesn't move. It feels stuck. Caught on something.

'Are you okay?' Patrick says as I put the phone down so I have both hands free to tackle the window. 'Imogen, you're worrying me. Are you okay?'

'I'm okay,' I grunt. 'This damn window won't budge.' It's only open a couple of inches and even when I try to push it back, it doesn't move. 'It won't budge,' I tell him. 'And I don't see how anyone could have got through a gap that size.'

'Maybe they used a hook or something to open the one next to it,' he says. 'Would that have been possible?'

I step back and look at the window frames a little more closely. If someone had an exceptionally long arm, or more likely some kind of stick and a fair amount of skill, then yes, they probably could have done it. I grasp the window again and yank it with all my strength. Finally, it closes. Breathless and trembling, I pick the phone back up and look at Patrick.

'I'm so sorry,' he says. 'I guess they waited until they saw my car leave and thought the place was empty. Has anything been taken?'

I'd been so absorbed with the notion of someone being in the house, I hadn't even thought about why they would be here. I sleep with my rings on and the rest of my jewellery is in a box in my beside table. Other than household appliances, there isn't much of value downstairs, particularly not in the kitchen. But I head back in there anyway and look in the open cupboards.

'I don't think so,' I reply.

'Well, that's good at least.'

'It doesn't change that someone was in our home when I was alone, sleeping in bed, Patrick.'

'You're right. It doesn't. I'm sorry. Look, I can come home tonight if that helps? And I'll get some of those alarms to go on all the windows too. And we can ring someone to come and set up a security system. A proper one.'

I nod, though it's purely in response to the security system and not to him coming home tonight. I'm not sure if that's what I want or not. What's worse – having to rely on your cheating husband or being in a house on your own where things like this can happen?

'I'll give you a ring later,' I say.

'Okay, do. Whatever you need. It's okay, Im. You don't need to worry.'

'Hmm.' I can't even respond with a word.

'We'll speak later, okay, I—'

I know exactly how he's going to finish that sentence, which is why I hang up before he can say those words. They don't mean anything any more.

32

With every cupboard I close, I search for some kind of clue. Some indication of who did this and why. As for the why, I think the answer is pretty clear – to cause as much torment as possible – and the who definitely points to the Springfield kids. If I wasn't so freaked out and angry, I'd probably find it laughable. All that effort I went to, moving away from that kind of life, and it's happening here, in this picturesque corner of the countryside. This is twisted. Maybe if they knew I was potentially pregnant, it would make a difference. Maybe that would put them off terrorising me. But considering they burnt down Maureen's shed – and she's a little old lady – I guess nobody is off-limits to them.

With a need to clear my head, I decide to focus the morning on painting. Though, when I step inside the studio, I discover it's not as easy as I'd thought.

There's not one gift waiting for me, but two. Both with cards on top. The smaller one is roughly wrapped, and it's clear from the clumsy job that it's an awkward shape. I rip off the note and read what's written inside. *It's not the most romantic gift, I'm afraid*, is all it says, scribbled in Patrick's handwriting. Intrigued, I pull off the wrapping and find a padlock – one to replace the old one he'd cut off the door. Putting that to the side, I take the other card off the second gift. *Felt like you needed something with a little more thought after the first unromantic gift*, it says. I unwrap the packaging and inside, I find a pair of earrings. Silver studs, with small diamonds in the centre. I say small, but they're probably half a caret and cost an absolute fortune. I'm one of those people who will wear the same pair of earrings for months, without changing them or taking them out, which is exactly what I plan on doing as I remove the ones I'm wearing and slip these in. Only as I attach the butterfly on the back, I hesitate. If they were bought out of love, it would have been an incredibly thoughtful gift, but if they're to distract me from what he's doing behind my back, then it's manipulative, and I want nothing to do with them. Then again, they're in now and Patrick is probably expecting me to wear them, so I keep them in.

Only now that I've got the padlock for the door do I realise how foolish it was to put all my materials in here last night with no way to secure them, and I'm strangely grateful that the wayward teens chose to come into the house, rather than in here. I can only imagine what they would have done if they'd got their hand on my art supplies. Nothing positive, that's for sure. I take the padlock out of the packaging and slip it over the latch, not that I think I'll forget to use it.

As I sit down at my seat, thoughts of Orla creep into my mind. With everything going on with Patrick, it wouldn't be hard to paint something melancholier, but that would feel almost like she's winning. So instead, I grab some alcohol paints and try something entirely new.

One of the things I loved most about art college was the experimentation. As soon as I got a name for myself, a style, that stopped happening so much. People had expectations, and I needed to stick to them. But right now, there's none of that, and I'm going to have fun. With my mind rolling through dozens of ideas, I start putting them down on paper.

When I'm working on a piece, nothing else matters. My mind stops whirring and I lose any ability to process time. Patrick finds it bizarre. More than once, he's walked in on me when I've been in the studio from first thing in the morning, and I don't notice him until he taps me on the shoulder and pulls me out of my trance.

'Did you stop for lunch?' he always says, already able to predict my answer.

'Is it lunchtime already?'

Sometimes he kisses me and shakes his head as if in disbelief, but more often he laughs.

'Lunch was hours ago. How do you not know that? Surely you must know how long you've been working on the painting for. It's almost finished.'

I see what he means, but it doesn't always work like that. Sometimes I can rework the smallest detail over and over for hours, while other times, just a few large, sweeping brushstrokes are all I need to complete an area. Time and art just don't go together. Not in a logical way, anyway. And believe me, for me to say something like that, it must be true.

I start with acrylics, but rather than reaching for a brush, I pull out a box with dozens of old rags I use for cleaning, mostly old T-shirts I bought second-hand from charity shops. I use the finest texture fabric to lay down a base coat, before doubling it up with a coarser, linen-type material. When I'm done with the T-shirts, I find more items to use, adding colour and texture as I go. Crushed paper, plastic water bottles, anything within my reach. I use my fingers too, smudging the work. Blurring the sharp lines and scraping my nails into thicker areas of paint. Sometimes I work with music on, but not today. Today, all I want is the silence in my head. Part way through, I switch medium, opting for charcoal, and it's only when long tendrils start spreading along the top of the canvas that I realise what it is I'm painting – a tree. A tree with a shadowy figure standing beside it.

I don't know how long I've been painting when I step back, but my hands have started to cramp. Still, I don't want to stop until I'm done. Not when everything is flowing so well.

'It's missing something,' I say to myself.

A problem for any artist can be knowing when to stop. You can go on forever adding improvements, changing little details, but they don't necessarily improve the work. I learned that long ago. But right now, this piece needs something a little extra. I feel a smile lift my expression as I realise what that is.

I take one of the heat guns off the side from where Orla placed them, only to swap it for a hairdryer instead. I fancy going old school with this. Back to my roots of not having much to work with. I've seen this technique where people dry the paint before it gets a chance to spread and it creates almost a topical map effect. It's a million miles from what I normally do, but right now, that's exactly what I want.

I grab a selection of colours – taupes, ochres, no hint of blues – and a couple of brushes, one of which I coat purely in water, which I sweep across the paper. Then I drop the ink directly onto it. I watch as the ink spread out. I'm going to want to add some metallics to it, I think as the movement slows. At which point I grab my hairdryer.

I switch it on, ready to dry my work, only for the entire thing to catch light.

33

It's not billowing out flames the way you'd imagine it happening in a cartoon. Instead, it's underneath the plastic. The area where the filament is. It's not just glowing though, it's actually caught fire.

'Shit, shit,' I say and instinctively pull at the plug. I don't even bother with the switch. I just yank it out from the wall. The instant I do, it stops and there's nothing but the sound of my hammering heart and the smell of burned plastic stinging my nose.

'What the fuck?' I stare at the object in my hand, trying to make sense of what I just saw. I have used tools a darn sight more powerful than a standard hairdryer hundreds of times and I've never experienced something like that. I've never even heard of something like that happening.

As my pulse tries to recover, my eyes shift to the plug socket. Could it be the electrics here? Other than the light switch, we didn't try any of them yesterday. Is it possible that water got into the sockets while we were cleaning? Would that have caused the hairdryer to overheat? I turn the plug over in my hand, trying to see if there's any sign of water. There isn't, but something else catches my attention. There's only one screw in the back of the plug. Where the second should be, to hold the case in place, there's nothing more than a hole. And even the screw that's in there isn't that secure.

Dropping it on the side, I go over to my boxes and rummage through them until I find what I'm looking for. A small screwdriver. I slip it into the remaining screw and twist it out of the plug. The plastic casing splits into two, exposing the electricals inside. I don't know what I'm looking for exactly. Everything's in place. Three wires and a fuse, and yet something feels off about it. I look at the half with the wires in for a minute longer, before looking at the plain plastic. There's writing stamped on it. *5A*, that's what it says. *5 Amps*. I've not fixed a lot of plugs in my life, but I still know what it means; this hairdryer needs a five-amp fuse to work in it. I double check the one in the plug only to find it's a much larger number – 13A. What does that mean? Should it work better with a higher fuse in?

I don't want to put the items down, but I know I have to, to get the answer I want. Carefully, so as not to disturb anything, I place both sides of the plug back on the side and open up my phone.

What would happen if you used a 13A fuse in a 5A hairdryer?

I already know what the answer is going to say. Something in the pit of my stomach has already told me. Still, my breath hitches as I read the words.

Using a 13A fuse would offer no protection. The device would effectively be short-circuited and a fire hazard.

No shit.

I look at the plug again. Did I do that? Did I put the wrong fuse in? No, I can't remember the last time I changed a fuse. Come to think of it, I can't remember where I got that hairdryer from either. In fact, now I look at it, I'm not sure I remember ever seeing it before, but if that's the case where would it have come from? How could a dangerous item have ended up in my studio?

The air in my lungs begins to wheeze. Someone planted it here. Someone wanted me to hurt myself with it. Or worse.

I can't stay in here any more. I can't. Standing up, I move towards the door and push on it to open, but it doesn't budge. I try again. And again, but it barely jangles.

I want to believe I'm wrong. Confused. The incident with the hairdryer has just left me shaken up, but as I use my shoulder and push harder, there's nothing. The padlock. The padlock is locked.

'This isn't funny!' I scream at the door. 'Whoever is doing this, it isn't funny. You need to let me out of here.' My breaths grow shallow as I bite down on the inside of my cheek, trying to control the fear rising through me. This is not the time to lose it. Not now. If these Springfield kids have been watching me, they know I live with Patrick. They might think he's coming home tonight. They might think he'll let me out. But he won't. I'll have to spend the night in here. In the cold, with no food, no water.

'I'm pregnant!' I scream. 'I'm pregnant and I'm calling the police. You need to let me out of here, because I'm pregnant and I'm calling the police and you are going to get in serious trouble.' I hammer my fists against the door, hitting it with such force that a spasm of pain shoots up my arm when, out of the corner of my eye, I catch a flash of movement somewhere out in the garden. I rush over to the window, craning my neck, trying to see who's out there, but there's nothing. I can't see anything.

Knowing that I need to make good on my threat, I pick up my phone, ready to dial 999. I force myself to empty my lungs before filling them with a deep inhale. In through the nose, with the intention of filling my lungs, but the air never gets that far. Because the first sniff is all it takes for me to smell it.

Smoke. Not the acrid smoke like I smelt after the plastic on the hairdryer started to melt. No, this is earthier and thick. This smells like wood or brick is on fire.

That's when it hits me. My studio is on fire. They're going to burn me alive in here.

34

They won't get here in time. That's all I can think. They won't get here in time.

I hold my phone limp in my hand, my mind frozen. My body unable to act. I don't know where the nearest fire station is – maybe fifteen minutes away at best. How long will it take for the flames to consume me in here? How long does it take fire to burn through damp brick? I don't know, but fifteen minutes has never felt so dangerously short.

'Think, Imogen!' My own voice helps to spur me into action. 'Move!' I can break the windows to get out. Yes, yes, that's definitely the best thing to do.

I pick up my stool and throw it into the window. The sound is deafening and the glass shatters outwards.

'Thank God,' I mutter, yet when I try to pull the stool back out, it won't budge. It's caught on the metal frames of the window. 'Shit! Fuck.' I grab hold of it with both hands and try to yank it out. The smell of smoke is getting thicker now. Cloying the back of my throat.

'I'm pregnant, you bastards!' I scream as I continue to tug at the stool. My eyes are blurring, but whether the tears are from fear or smoke, I can't tell. With one final yank, I free the stool, but it's left jagged shards of glass sticking out along the bottom of the frame.

If I climb out to save myself from the fire only to sever an artery, I'll be no better off.

I need to slow down and think. I can hear the metal creaking as the heat of the fire forces it to expand against its will, but the flames haven't reached the window yet. I have time to think, and what I need to do is get rid of the glass. Without a second's thought, I grab one of my cleaning rags, wrap it around my fist, and start knocking out the shards of glass until there's a gap big enough for me to climb through. It's not going to be nice, and I won't get away unscathed, but I can do it.

I put my leg on the stool, ready to hoist myself over, when I hear a strange hissing sound. Is the door about to cave in and the flames engulf me? Am I going to die here seconds away from freedom? No. I won't let that happen. I have to get out of here.

'Imogen? Are you in there? It's all right, love. I've got you. Hang on!'

'Maureen?' I gasp, my throat raw.

'It's all right, I'm putting it out now. I'm on it.'

My lungs shudder as I expel a staggered breath of relief so great my whole body shakes. The hissing wasn't the door about to implode; it was the sound of the extinguisher. Crazy, paranoid Maureen with all her fire extinguishers.

'I don't know if I should climb out,' I say, my voice wobbling. And it's only when I go to brush my face that I realise tears are streaming down it. 'I could climb out, but... I think I'm pregnant. I think I'm pregnant, Maureen. I need to get out of here. I *need* to get out.'

'Don't you worry, it's nearly out. It's nearly out,' she calls back. A minute later I hear her rattling the door. 'Bugger me, that's hot,' she mutters before the door swings open. I can't even run to her. Instead, I drop to the ground and weep.

'I've got you, I've got you,' she says, stroking my head like I'm a child. 'You're safe now.'

'I thought I was going to die.'

'I know you did, love, but you're safe now. Those fucking kids. Well, this time we've got 'em. They'll go to jail for this. You mark my words.'

35

'You sit there and you drink this,' Maureen says, placing a mug of tea on the side table next to me. She guided me back to her house and I didn't put up any objection. The Springfield kids have got me in their sights now, not her. 'Got plenty of sugar in it. I think you're gonna need it. You've had a nasty shock there.'

Nasty shock? That's the understatement of the year. 'They tried to kill me,' I say. 'They set fire to the studio while I was inside it. And they knew I was in there. They had to have known I was in there.'

Maureen doesn't say anything, but I can't blame her. What can you say? Instead, she breathes deeply, her chest rising and falling as Brutus sits beside her, resting his head on her lap.

'How did you know?' I say after a moment. 'How did you know I was in there? Did you see them? Did you see them running off?'

She shakes her head and looks down at the dog. 'Not me – him. Started acting all funny. Barking and growling and stuff. Bit like he did that night. And then I heard you screaming. That's when I got my extinguisher. People thought I was crazy for putting it outside my front door, but I knew I wasn't. I knew I'd need it if they tried something like that again.'

'Thank you,' I say, though to be honest, it doesn't feel sufficient for her just saving my life. Besides, she's not the only one I need to thank.

'Thank you, Brutus. I don't know what I would've done if you hadn't heard them.'

'Well, I think we both know the answer to that one,' Maureen says solemnly.

We do. The thought causes my breath to constrict. If Maureen hadn't come, would I have made it out alive? I certainly wouldn't be unscathed, if I can call myself that now. My body may look fine, but my mind is going to take a while to catch up. Trying to breathe deeply, I pick up my tea and take a sip.

Maureen wasn't joking about the sugar. I think she measured it in tablespoons rather than teaspoons, but still, I'm grateful nonetheless.

'We should ring the police,' I say when I put the cup down. 'We should ring the police. They need to come. They need to take evidence.'

'It's all right, love. I'm on it. I've already texted Donny.'

'Donny? He's the one who dealt with them before?'

I try not to sound so sceptical. I'm sure he did what he could, but if he'd done a better job, I wouldn't have been fearing for my life only half an hour ago.

'Yes. He knows what's going on and he wants these buggers behind bars as much as we do. Besides, he's high up. Not one of those uniform types – they take forever to get things sorted. I've told him what happened, and he's said he'll be over quick as. Probably twenty minutes or so.'

'Thank you, thank you.'

'You can wait here till he comes. I made a venison stew last night, but don't suppose you'll be wanting any of that, will you?'

I let out a brief chuckle. It feels strange to laugh, like my throat isn't sure it's meant to make that type of sound any more.

'No, I'll pass on that. I'm just fine with the tea.'

'Well, I'll see if I can find some biscuits to go with it. You stay here with her, Brutus. I think she needs a bit of your company.'

Despite Maureen's request, Brutus promptly trots after his owner into the kitchen, leaving me with my sweet tea and a head full of questions I can't make sense of.

How the hell did that just happen? How... why... who would do something like that? I don't care what Maureen said about kids being bored and needing some entertainment. That's not entertainment. That's murder. Whoever these Springfield lads are, they are sick. At least I know who did that thing with the cupboards this morning. And who switched out the fuse in my hairdryer. As I consider the torment inflicted on me over the last twenty-four hours, another memory sparks.

They were watching me. They had to have been, to sneak into the house and open all the cupboards between Patrick leaving and me waking up. So maybe they were watching me in town, too. Maybe they were the ones who stuck the drawing pins into my bike tyre. Have they been following me since we got here? I think of the shadowy figure standing outside in the field. How was that only two nights ago? It feels like everything has changed since then.

As I take another sip of my tea, I hear Maureen talking.

'Of course she's shaken up. Who wouldn't be? Yeah, don't worry, I know. You don't need to tell me... Stop using that tone. I said I know. Fine. We'll speak later.'

With that, the conversation ends, and an unexpected unease

prickles my skin, though before it can settle she walks into the room.

'Everything okay?' I ask.

'It was just Donny telling me not to touch things. Like I don't know that. But he's closer than I thought, so that's good. Another ten minutes. And I managed to find some squashed fly biscuits.'

'Squashed fly?' I say. I try not to look too horrified, but after the pheasants on the gatepost, I'm terrified that's actually what's in them.

'Garibaldis. Don't tell me you've never called them that before!' She laughs.

I chuckle as I take a biscuit. 'No, no, I haven't, but thank you.'

I take my biscuit and dunk it into my tea.

We fall into silence, and for a minute, I assume we're going to stay that way until Donny turns up. But then Maureen speaks, far more softly than I've heard her speak before.

'You said you're pregnant? I guess that's the reason for no wine, then?'

I dip my chin into a nod. 'I think so. I mean... Patrick and I are trying. We had IVF. I'm not meant to do a test until tomorrow, but I've been feeling sick and I feel... I don't know... different.'

'Sounds to me like you might be, then. Never had any kids myself,' she says. 'But I was quite close to my sister. She had a few – said she knew straight away. Could feel it in her bones. Don't think she even bothered doing a pregnancy test with the second one.'

'Wow.'

I'm about to ask her where her sister and niece or nephew are when there's the sound of a car rattling out on the lane. All of a sudden, Brutus starts wagging his tail.

'I guess that must be Donny,' Maureen says, standing up. 'I guess I should let him in.'

36

Without realising, I'd already formed an image of Donny in my head. Middle-aged, middle-class, perhaps with a slight paunch that television shows deem stereotypical for plainclothes police officers. But the man who walks in through the door looks nothing like that.

His head is shaved bald, and there are several tattoos on his hands, fingers, and even his neck. Maybe it's wrong of me, but I'd assumed there would be some kind of rules about working in the police with tattoos like that. I guess I'm wrong. And let's be honest, if I were a criminal, I'd be far more scared of someone who looked like they could easily and happily throw me off the roof of a building than someone who looks like they spend all day sitting behind a desk eating donuts. It also shifts my perception of the type of people who live in this quaint area of the countryside. For someone who grew up with everyone making assumptions based on where I'd come from, I should probably do better than make assumptions of my own – but it's difficult.

'Auntie Mo,' he says when he comes in.

'You're related?' I can't hide the shock in my voice, though Maureen immediately shakes her head and laughs.

'No, everyone around here calls me that. It's what you get when you've lived alone as long as me.' Her laughter stops as she turns her attention back to Donny. 'They set fire to a shed, just like they did with mine. Only this time, she was in it.'

'It's an art studio, not a shed,' I say, feeling some strange urge to correct her. 'And they locked me inside.'

Donny's eyebrow rises. 'They locked you in? They locked you in before they set fire to it? And they definitely knew you were in there?'

I nod. 'I'm sure they did. That isn't the only thing they've done. They were in my house this morning. Messing with the cupboards. And they changed a fuse so my hairdryer caught fire. I think they wanted it to look like an electrical accident, but when that didn't work, they set light to the studio instead. It's attempted murder, right? They can't just get away with it. They can't.'

Donny narrows his eyes. 'Trust me, if I had my way, they would've been behind bars years ago. But the Springfields... it's not just the money – they've got all sorts of power behind them. Lawyers in the family—'

'I don't care if they've got lawyers in the family. My goddamn husband is a lawyer! They need to go to prison for this.'

He stops and nods slowly. 'No, you're right. You're right. I'll go round, take a few photos, pass it up. I'll go down there myself. Make sure we get a proper investigation on this one.'

'Thank you, thank you,' I say. 'I'll give you whatever information I can. It started as soon as I got here. One of them was watching me from out in the field on the very first night, and I'm pretty sure they punctured the tyre on my bike. It all feels like too much to be a coincidence.'

'Watching you at night?' Donny looks at Maureen as I say this.

She shrugs. 'I don't know anything about that?' she says.

'Maybe we should talk to Patrick about it,' Donny suggests.

I grit my teeth. I *fucking* hate comments like that, where men assume the 'man of the house' knows more. As if we're still stuck in the past when women couldn't even own property. A house doesn't need a man in it and even if it has one, what good is he going to be when he didn't see anything?

'I can tell you everything you need to know,' I snap.

Donny nods and pulls out his phone, probably to make a note. 'I'll look into it, but this really sounds like the Springfield lads' MO.'

He looks as if he's about to leave, but before he does, Maureen speaks again.

'She's pregnant, you know,' she says. 'They tried to kill her, and she's pregnant. They could get double life for that, couldn't they? The police should charge them properly, right? Double.'

Donny looks at the old woman, a slight glare in his eye. I get the impression that making police suggestions is something Maureen's done a lot to him.

'Don't you worry about that stuff, Mo. That's my job in all this, remember?'

She sniffs dismissively before she nods. 'Fine, fine. Well, you should go get your photos of the crime scene. You go straight up there. I need to know you're onto them.'

With yet another resigned nod, Donny turns to me.

'Do you need anything? I'll go to the farm straight after here and let them know I'm watching them. They would have to be insane to try anything again tonight. But if you want to stay the night in a hotel, maybe that'd be a good idea. You could always decide once Patrick's home.'

I'm about to ask how he knows Patrick's name, but then so did Maureen when we first arrived here. I guess it's just how it is in the countryside.

'He's working at the minute. But he's coming back tonight,' I say, reminding myself that I still haven't confirmed that with him. Earlier, I hadn't known if I needed him to be with me or if I was able to just push through, but after this incident I'm done. I want my husband home. Work will have to come second. 'I'll ask him what he wants to do.'

'Good. That'll be good. Get my number from Mo, just in case you need to ring me.'

I nod. 'Will do.'

A moment later, he's gone.

37

It's only when Donny leaves that I realise he didn't actually ask where to go, but I guess that's not that surprising. Just like with Patrick's name, everybody knows everything here and there's a good chance that Maureen told him a lot of the details on the phone. After all, I wasn't in a great place to listen when she first brought me in here.

Without asking, Maureen picks up my mug and goes to refill it.

'Guess we should probably give him half an hour or so,' she says. 'Do you want to give Patrick a ring? I'll just let Brutus out the back if you need some space?'

'Thank you.' I nod. With a slight smile, she whistles sharply and Brutus runs to the back door. As they step outside, I take out my phone and hold it in my hand.

I didn't want to need Patrick. I wanted to prove that I could manage without him. And under normal circumstances, I would be able to. But this is not a normal circumstance. I nearly lost my life. It doesn't make me weak to want someone by my side while the police investigate this. Even if the person beside me is a lying cheat. A lying cheat that I love with all my heart.

I've heard it said that people cheat for a reason, and sometimes that reason is simply they're a vile human with no emotional intelligence, but I don't believe that about Patrick. Maybe I missed something. Maybe there is a reason he's done this to me, and maybe... hopefully, we can work through it. That's what I want to do, I realise. I want to know why he's done this and, if we can, I want to work through it. I want to raise our child in the type of family that I never had. I just hope he wants that too.

With my heart in my throat, I hit dial. It takes a couple of rings before he picks up.

'Hey, I was going to ring you in a bit,' he says. 'How are you doing?'

'They set fire to the studio.'

'What?'

'The Springfield kids. They set fire to the studio while I was in it. They locked me in.'

I hear his gasp reverberate down the line. 'What the hell, Im? What? I'm coming home now.'

The relief of his words billows through me, though I respond almost reflexively. 'You don't need to do that. The police are at the house now. Donny, the one who investigated before. And I'm with Maureen.'

'You're with Maureen? And you're sure you're safe?'

'She was the one who got me out with her fire extinguisher,' I tell him.

'She did?'

'Yeah. Thank God she was there.'

'Fuck... Shit... But you're okay, right? Do you need to go to hospital?'

'No, I'm all right. I'm okay,' I say, though my pulse is once again so high it's hard to believe that's true. As I struggle to know how to carry the conversation on, tears fill my eyes.

'You know I love you more than anything, don't you?'

'Of course I do, and I feel the same.'

'And I'd never do anything to hurt you. I'm so sorry you had to go through that, Im. I'm so sorry I wasn't there for you.'

It's not exactly the answer I was hoping for but it's the same sentiment, at least.

'Look, let me see how quickly I can get all this work done and I'll be home as soon as I can, okay? Just take care of yourself, all right? You have to take care of yourself. I love you.'

'I love you too.'

A moment later, the line is dead, and I sit there, staring at my phone screen. Patrick loves me. I know that. And it isn't just a case of the words he said. I heard the fear and pain in his voice. The pure panic that I could be hurt. Whoever he was talking to yesterday on the phone, I've got my wires crossed. I must have.

I place the phone down on the arm of the chair and wipe my cheeks with the back of my hands. Part of me already regrets telling Patrick he didn't need to come straight home as now I either have to stay at Maureen's until he gets here or face the house alone, and I'm not sure which is preferable. There has to be a third option, but before I can think what it is, the door swings open and Maureen and Brutus walk back into the house.

Her expression is pinched in a frown and her lips are so tightly pursed that a thousand wrinkles stretch out from them.

'I think I made a mistake,' she says quietly. 'I think I did something bad.'

38

As Maureen stands there, Brutus continues to wag his tail, but she doesn't so much as reach a hand down to him. Instead, her eyes are locked solely on me.

'What is it? Are you okay?' I ask.

She shakes her head. 'I was outside, and I could hear Donny on the phone, talking about the studio and things, and it got me thinking about the padlock. It was hot, you see, I couldn't touch it. So I needed something to grip it with, so I used my scarf to get a hold, but now I'm wondering if that was a bad idea. I mean, they won't be able to get any fingerprints off it, will they? That's evidence I've destroyed. People get in trouble for destroying evidence, don't they?'

I don't know whether I should laugh or cry. She's right, fingerprints on the padlock might well have been the exact evidence we needed to put them away, but she also sounds worried that she might get in trouble for destroying evidence. Given that I wouldn't be alive if she hadn't, I'm bloody glad she did.

'I suspect they used gloves,' I say. 'Besides, there'll be other places they can get fingerprints from, like the hairdryer that they tampered with.'

She nods, but she looks only partly assured by my words. 'They should have gone away last year,' she says. 'If I'd put up more of a fuss, gone to the papers maybe...'

'I'm sure you did everything you could,' I say, walking over to her and placing a hand on her arm. 'You are not to blame for any of this.'

'I just hate it. Wherever you go, there's always someone with all the power. When I grew up, it was the Ridings. Nasty folk, they were. Every family was terrified of getting in their bad books. They owned a lot of businesses, you see, and if they didn't like you, you couldn't get a job. I didn't grow up somewhere like here though, no. It was gangs and thugs where I was.'

'Sounds like where I grew up,' I say.

Her eyes meet mine and a slight smile twists on the corner of her mouth. 'Ah, well, then you get it. You just had to keep your head down and get on with your life. Then, if you were lucky, they'd leave you alone, let you get by. But the Springfields, they're like a different breed. I mean, their family isn't just rich, they're smart. They've got influence high up. And if this is what they're like when you haven't crossed them, I hate to imagine what they're like if you do.'

A shudder ripples through my spine. It feels like something in a bad mafia movie, where I've moved in on someone else's turf without knowing. But I'm not going to let it beat me. I refuse to.

I draw in a long breath and look Maureen square in the eye.

'I meant what I said to Donny. Patrick is a lawyer, and he's not going to let this go. We are going to put everything behind this to make sure those Springfield kids never terrorise you or me or anyone else again. They picked the wrong people to mess with.'

This time her smile holds a little steadier before it transforms into a chuckle.

'What? What did I say?' I ask.

'Nothing,' she says, her laughter continuing. 'I just never thought I'd meet a vegetarian I actually like.'

39

It's only when Maureen offers to cook me something – another jacket potato – that I get the impression she doesn't want me to stay here solely for my own benefit. I hadn't really thought about it until now, but she's obviously been shaken up by the incident too. She just had to put out a fire in a room with a possibly pregnant woman inside. That can't have been easy to go through, especially not when she's still dealing with her own trauma from when her shed was set on fire. She clearly needs someone here to talk to, to comfort her a little, and I'm torn. There's still something about her that I find unnerving. Sometimes, it feels like she can't quite meet my eye. And then there's Brutus. One word from her and I swear he'd rip my throat out. But she saved my life. I wouldn't be here without her. If that's not worth spending a couple of hours a day getting to know her, then I don't know what is.

'So you and Donny are close?' I ask. 'You must be if he called you Auntie Mo?'

'Well, actually he looked at the house same time I did, but he ended up getting a place in the village up the road.'

'How did you end up here? You said it's not like where you grew up? And your accent, it's from up north, right?'

'Manchester, born and bred. Thought I'd be there forever, but then I got some insurance money and, well, now I'm here.'

My immediate response is to ask what the insurance money was for, but I hold back. It doesn't seem the neighbourly thing to do.

'And what about Donny? He has family in the village too, I assume? What do they do?'

'Oh, Donny's all about family. Very much. Everything he does is for family. They're very lucky to have a man like that looking after them.'

The way she speaks is almost a gush, as if she's personally proud of the man Donny is, though I can't imagine she has much influence there. Then again, if he moved here nearly twenty years ago, he must have been in his early twenties. Most of the houses in the village cost well over half a million. I've always known that police officers have good pensions, but I didn't realise the salaries were good enough to afford a mortgage like that. Then again, who's to say his wife isn't the primary earner in the family?

Ten minutes or so after I hear Donny's car driving away, I make my excuses.

'I should go back. Like Donny said, there's no chance they'll be stupid enough to try something tonight, and I don't want Patrick to worry if he comes home and I'm not there.'

'Well, you know where I am if you change your mind,' she says. 'And this has been nice. Not the first part, but talking to you. Getting to know you. I've enjoyed it.'

'Yes, so have I.'

'And don't worry, Donny will see to it. He's never let us down yet.'

The fact the local pyromaniacs are still at large means I don't entirely agree with Maureen's statement, but I don't say anything. Instead, I give her a quick hug.

As I go to leave, my gaze falls on the fire extinguisher on the windowsill. It's one of three in the room. Another is next to the fireplace while a third is just beside the door.

'Maureen,' I say. 'You wouldn't mind if I took one of your extinguishers, would you? Just until I get one of my own. You know, in case they come again.'

'Of course not,' she says, striding over and picking up the one that I was looking at. 'Now, you'll want to remember to PASS when you use it.'

'Sorry?'

'PASS. Pull out the pin, aim, squeeze and sweep. It's a handy little acronym.'

'Pull out pin, aim, squeeze and sweep,' I repeat while imagining myself doing the actions. 'Thank you, Maureen. I really appreciate this.'

'Well, I just hope you don't have to use it.' The old lady smiles sadly.

'Me too,' I say. 'Me too.'

As I walk home, the cold air bites at my skin. Today is the antithesis of yesterday in terms of weather. Grey clouds and no evidence of a sun behind them at all. I can't believe it's only been two days since we moved here. How can so much happen in two days? And it's not likely to get any calmer either. At some point, the police will want to question me properly and then there's the pregnancy to think of. It might be two more days until I'm meant to do the test, but with each passing hour it feels more and more a forgone conclusion that I'm pregnant. Like Maureen said about her sister, it's almost as though I can feel it in my bones.

I try to focus on that – on the good things waiting for me in the future, and there will be plenty. I know that. Yet as I glance at my new home, my mind flashes back to the moment: to the memory of my shoulder pushing against the door and finding it shut, to that first whiff of smoke that I swear is still clinging to the back of my throat. I no longer think Maureen is completely crazy for repainting her home. I get it. That smell lingers, and with it, the memories I'd rather forget.

I don't bother opening the gate; instead, I just slip around the gap by the side. Until this moment, I hadn't even thought about how I was going to get into the house – I don't have my keys; I left them in the house while I was working in the studio. But I did leave the back door unlocked.

I'm not too keen on seeing the studio black with smoke, especially when just the sight of the house was enough to cause a flashback, but there's no way around it. I either go around the back of the house or I go back to Maureen's. At least, that's what I think, until I step onto the path and freeze.

My throat tightens and the goosebumps that rise on my arms have nothing to do with the cold. There's no need to go around the back at all. The front door is currently three inches open.

40

I can hear my heart hammering against my ribcage. My throat is drying so fast it makes it impossible to swallow.

I didn't go out through the front door. I know I didn't. I haven't been out the front of the house all day, and it wasn't open this morning. I checked when I was searching for the way those arseholes got into the house overnight. The door was definitely locked, and yet now it is three inches open, and I can't draw my eyes away.

Could it be Donny? Donny doesn't have a key to the house, and why would he even need to go in? The fire was out the back. He could have let himself in through the open door at the back and walked through to the front, but why? Maybe to have seen if there was anyone in the house? It's possible.

Then again, maybe Patrick came home earlier than expected? I dismiss the thought almost as quickly as it forms. Patrick drove to the station, meaning he'd drive back. There's no sign of his car. So, what?

A thick lump wedges itself in my throat. I can't hear any sounds coming from inside, but that doesn't mean there isn't someone in there. Or worse. Several people. The question is, how many? Maureen constantly referred to the group of arsonists as 'the Springfield kids' but she never put a number on how many there were.

I inch forward, only to stop myself. Do I really want to go in there? Do I really want to walk into my house with the possibility of facing any number of intruders, when only two hours before I feared for my life?

No, I don't. But maybe I should. Maybe this is the evidence I need – catching them trespassing – to put them away for good. I put the fire extinguisher down, then I take my phone out and switch it onto video. As I press record, I hold my phone out in front of me before I take another step forward and pull the door open all the way.

'I know you're in there!' I shout. 'I know you're trying to scare me. And it won't work.'

I wait, arm stretched into the hallway as I sweep my phone from side to side while I strain to listen for any noise. But there's nothing. Nothing but the silence of the house.

Still, my pulse doesn't lower as I take a step inside. The floor creaks beneath my feet, and I tighten my grip on the phone. There's nothing. No one's here. Donny must have left the door open. That's what I think until a single thud echoes through from the back of the house and all the way into my bones.

My stomach lurches and I want to run, but I need to catch them. I need to have the proof of what they've been doing.

'I've called the police!' I yell. 'The police know what you've done, and they're going to arrest you.'

There's another thud, one after another, and with my heart performing somersaults, I understand exactly what the sounds are. They're footsteps. There's no doubt in my mind. Someone is here.

'You need to get off my property,' I say, bellowing with a strength I don't feel. 'Get off my property now. My husband is a lawyer, and you are going to go down for a very long time, believe me.'

My heart is hammering so hard it has to be bruising my chest, while my pulse is beating against my eardrums with such force it takes me a moment to realise that the footsteps have stopped. I hold my breath, not sure what to do next, when, without warning, the door to the living room swings open.

The figure who appears is a head taller than me, but their build is slight, though it's their face I can't draw my eyes away from.

'Come on, you're going to use the "my husband's a lawyer" line on me? Really?' A smirk rises on their face. 'That's my dad you're talking about.'

41

She is a strikingly attractive young woman. I've always thought that. She's got Patrick's height, but Arabella's slight frame and dark hair. Her eyes are a light hazel, so light they look like melted amber, while her skin is a beautiful golden brown – although unlike the hair and eye colour, I'm certain that part comes from a bottle. White teeth, red lips. It's no wonder she's got so many people wrapped around her finger, but all I want to do is smack her in the face.

'What the hell are you doing in my house?' I hiss, stepping inwards and ending the recording on my phone before I drop my hand.

'Well, that's not a nice reaction to give your favourite step-daughter. I thought you'd be pleased to see me.'

'How long have you been here? When did you arrive?'

She shrugs. 'Oh, I've been here a little while now. I've just been hanging out. Getting to know the new haunt.'

A little while?

'Was it you?' My temperature drops as I stride towards her. 'Did you do it? Did you just try to kill me?'

I shake my head as I try to make my thoughts align. It would make sense. She could have let herself in through the front door with her key this morning and opened all the cupboards, just to unnerve me. Then when the hairdryer trick didn't work and start a fire the way she had envisioned, she went for the less subtle approach of setting it alight herself. I lunge for her, trying to grab the back of her jacket so I can hurl her out the way she came.

'What the hell?' she says, pushing me off her. 'What the fuck is wrong with you?'

'Get out of my house. I *know* you did it. I know you did it all!'

'What are you on about? I only got here five minutes ago. Five minutes. That's it.'

'Then where's your car?'

'I got a taxi from the station! It dropped me at the end of the lane. I didn't think it would be such a bloody walk.'

'I don't believe you.' I'm still trying to get a hold of her, but she keeps moving. She's in the kitchen now. In the part of the house she'd been in this morning when she'd given me the first scare of the day. It makes sense why I didn't see anyone coming through the garden when they lit the fire, too. She would have just let herself in through the front door again, assuming she even left the house. She could have been hiding inside one of the spare rooms all day. Watching me. The thought makes me want to vomit.

I step back, my lips curling up in a snarl.

'The police came, you know. They came and took evidence. You'll go to prison for it. It's attempted murder. Your dad won't be able to stop it. He won't want to. You've pushed it too far this time. He'll disown you.'

Prim's the one shaking her head and laughing. 'I don't know what you're on about, but you're crazy,' she says.

'No, I'm not. Now, give me your keys.' I lunge for her again, this time grabbing at her pockets. 'Give me my key back!'

'Get your fucking hands off me,' she says, but I don't. I don't let her go. She twists and pushes me back, and for someone so slight, she's a lot stronger than she looks.

'My dad's going to hear about this,' she hisses. 'I always knew you were mental, but this is insane. You crazy bitch, get away from me!'

'Give me my key back!'

I go to grab her, but she swings her arm, and her fist catches me across the jaw. I topple to the side, catching myself with my hands before I hit the countertop. If I'd been a split second later, I would have hit my stomach. I would have hit my baby.

I spin round to face Prim, my face glowing with heat.

'You lay a hand on me or my baby again, and I swear to God, it will be me who goes to prison and you will be in the ground. You get that? I don't care. I'll do it. You hurt us again, and I will end your life.'

Prim backs away. For the first time since I found her in my house, there's a flash of fear on her face. Finally, she's heard me. She can see I'm not joking. That I'm going to make her accountable for what she's done.

But as she opens her mouth, the words stutter from her lips. 'No... you can't be pregnant,' she says. 'You can't. He wouldn't do that. He wouldn't do that to us.'

42

All her bravado is gone. She looks like she's about to cry. In fact, I'm almost certain that she is. Her eyes are glazed with tears as her bottom lip trembles ever so slightly.

'You're lying,' she says, her voice quivering. 'You're doing this to manipulate him. He wouldn't do that. He wouldn't have a baby with you.'

'What? You don't believe that. You can't.' I take a breath, trying to steady myself. I'm still fucking furious, but I'm also in pure disbelief. 'We've had IVF, Prim. We've been going through it for months now. It was your father's idea. You know, to move things along quickly, because that's what he wants. That's what we both want. A family. I thought he told you that?'

When the conversation of IVF first came up, I asked Patrick how he was going to let Prim know he was intending on starting a family with me, and his answer was somewhere along the lines of 'I'll handle it'. I had thought little about it at the time. She's his daughter, not mine. I assumed he would know the best way to approach it with her. Apparently, he went for the evasion technique. I suspect he wanted to wait until we'd actually conceived, which makes sense in a lot of ways. Except now I'm the one having to break the news to a very angry, very unstable young woman.

'It's very early on. I'm sure he was going to tell you soon,' I say, not sure why I'm trying to comfort her. Not when there's still a bloody good chance she was behind the fire.

Her lip stops trembling, and her jaw locks into place. The tears in her eyes vanish, replaced by a burning rage.

'Why?' she hisses. 'Why did you have to come into our lives? They were happy before you. They loved each other before you. You ruined everything.'

'It's not about you,' I say, shaking my head at her obtuse naivety. I know she was at boarding school, but surely she would have seen the cracks in her parents' relationship? 'Your mother made him miserable. She controlled his life.'

'No! No!' Her voice cracks. 'She didn't! They were a team. He doted on her. He *always* doted on her. She loved him, and he adored her. Everything was perfect, and then you messed it up!'

It's bizarre. I'm standing in front of a grown woman – twenty-one years of age – and physically, she looks like an adult. But the way she's speaking is like a small child who just wants their parents to stay together forever and won't accept that they're their own people with their own feelings to consider.

For a second, I feel a pang of sympathy towards her. Maybe I would have felt that way if my parents had actually been together. If I had any memories of the three of us, then maybe I would've found it hard to let go, too. But as sad as it is to see Prim like this, my loyalty doesn't lie with her. It lies with Patrick, and regardless of our current bump in the road, I know he's 100 per cent happier with Arabella out of his life and me in it.

'Look, I get that this is hard for you. Change is always hard.

But this baby, it's going to be your sibling. A little brother or sister.'

'No!' She shakes her head fiercely. 'No, it can't be. He still loves her. I know he still loves her.'

'Prim, surely you want your dad to be happy?'

'He was happy with *her*!' Tears spill down her cheeks. 'He was always happy with her. I know she wasn't easy... She has her dark days, her down days, but everyone has them now and again. She's been through a lot. He was supposed to stay by her side through it all. He was supposed to stay with her!'

It takes all my restraint not to laugh at the thought of Arabella's down days. I can only imagine they stem from things like not being able to get a last-minute reservation at her favourite restaurant or snapping a designer heel.

Still, I've seen a lot of sides to Prim since her father and I got together two years ago. The socialite Prim. The spoiled, self-centred Prim. The malicious, conniving, jealous Prim. But I've never seen this side – the heartbroken Prim. The vulnerable Prim.

'I never wanted us to be against one another, Prim,' I say quietly. 'All I've ever wanted is for your dad to be happy.'

She scoffs. 'You don't even know him well enough to make him happy. He proposed after four months. Don't you think that's strange? I've had relationships longer than that. Actually, all of my relationships have been longer than that, and I wouldn't have agreed to marry any of them.'

'It's different when you're older—'

'You're closer to my age than his, for fuck's sake!' Her head drops and I think about stepping towards her, but I hesitate, and when she looks back up at me, her lip is curled, ready for another cutting remark.

'He bought her a ring, you know. An eternity ring. Two weeks before he left her.'

'What?'

'He gave Mum an eternity ring. Platinum. Dozens of diamonds. It must have cost a fortune. More than your engagement ring. She still wears it now. She still wears all of her rings.'

'That's her prerogative,' I say, trying not to let the comment sting. It's not a reflection on Patrick or me or our relationship. It's Arabella again, trying to control the situation, or at least the parts that she can be in control of. Which, right now, looks like Prim.

'Right? But why? Why would he do that? Why would he do that, unless, on some level, he knew he would end up with her? I think that's why he did it. Because he knew. He knew, deep down, that you and he wouldn't last. You are a fling, a bit of fun, and when he grows tired of it, he'll go back to her, and she'll have him. Because that's the way real love works. Not whatever this is you're playing at.'

I bite the inside of my cheeks, stopping myself from saying something I'll regret. Not that I don't think she deserves it, but this is Patrick's daughter, my child's half-sister, and whatever is going on with us at the moment, I need to remember not to do anything irreversible. Still, it doesn't stop the jangle of jealousy in my chest, and the memory of the night before rushes into my mind: Patrick, telling someone on the phone that he'd love them forever. If he wasn't talking to Prim, then maybe it was Arabella?

I shake the idea away. It's preposterous, and I'm not being pulled into her games. Instead, I draw in a long breath.

'Your mum might still wear all her rings,' I say, 'but your dad only wears one. The one I gave him on our wedding day. The one that says "Love always", because that's what we promised to do for one another. So I'm sorry if this hurts you, because you being hurt means your father is hurt too, and that is one thing I never want to happen. But this is my house, and if you come back here again, I will call the police.'

Prim's eyes narrow as her lips form that all-too-familiar sneer.

'Don't worry, I wasn't planning on staying. Why the hell would anyone want to stay in a shithole like this?'

She moves to push past me and leave, but I grab her by the top of her arm.

'The key, Prim? I want my key.'

With a huff, she pulls her keyring out of her bag, fiddles with it for a minute, then slams the key down on the table before locking eyes with me.

'You'll regret doing this – getting in between my family. You and your baby both will.'

'Are you threatening me?' I say. 'Because if you are, then please keep going. It's all the more evidence for me to take to the police.'

She scoffs. 'Oh, I'm not threatening you. I'm just preparing you.'

43

As the door slams shut, I drop onto the dining chair. My head falls into my hands as my heart continues to pound. What the hell is going on? I should have known how Prim would react to the pregnancy, and it probably wasn't a wise idea for me to speak to her on my own, without Patrick there – especially not when I haven't done the test yet. But then, I never would have ended up in this situation had Patrick not given her a key. Or if he'd actually discussed with her how we were trying for a baby together, the way he told me he was going to.

I grab a glass of water in the hope it might alleviate the throbbing behind my temples, but I don't hold out much hope. I'm not sure how much of this pain is purely physical and how much is my body reacting to all this stress. It's probably a combination of both.

Checking my watch, I see it's almost five o'clock. The day has disappeared, and other than the cup of tea and the squashed fly biscuits at Maureen's, I've not eaten anything. My stomach growls angrily, but I don't move. All that's in the fridge is the old antipasto from the night before, and I can't bear the thought of going out of the house again. It's not like it's a long drive to the supermarket. It's just that every time I leave, something else happens, and I'm not sure I can cope with any more. What I want to do is wait until Patrick comes home, drop onto his shoulder, and let out all the tears I've been holding inside. But I don't know when he's going to be home, so instead, I head into the living room with a sketchbook and wait.

The drawings I come up with are shadowed and heavy. Bending trees, blurred figures and flames creeping in at the edges. It's only a sketch, a minute image of what I'm actually going to create, but Orla wanted dark and that's definitely what she's going to get here. Not that I'm going to show it to Orla. No, she burned her bridges with me when she pretended to be visiting out of friendship. Maybe if she'd been honest when she arrived it would have been something we could have worked through, but all that helpfulness was just manipulation, and I do not take well to being manipulated.

With one sketch down, I move onto the next and then another. A bubble of pride rises within me. This collection is going to be one of the best I've created. I can feel it, and I'm half-tempted to go into the studio and make a start on it, only I remember the broken window, the smoke-stained door, and the fact that I don't want to leave the house until Patrick comes home. So instead, I keep going, leaving some pages only half scrawled on, and completing far more detailed outlines on others. When I glance at my phone, I'm surprised to see how late it is. It's already half past seven, and outside is completely dark. I've spent over two hours just scribbling away. Patrick said he was going to get home as soon as he could finish up, but what time is that going to be? He wanted to stay in London to work late and with Patrick that means gone midnight. He wouldn't stay there until then, would he? Not when he knows what I've been through.

The mild respite that drawing brought me ebbs away. The silence of the house wraps around the walls. In my mind, I see the image standing out in the field. Are they there now, watching me? Why didn't I do as Donny said and check into a hotel? It's not too late to go, of course, but then Patrick might be nearly home. I pick up my phone and call him.

'Hey, gorgeous, I've just got into the car.' He answers my question without me needing to ask it, and it's impossible not to feel relieved. 'I wanted to get away sooner, but I'll be twenty minutes at most. Unless you want me to pick up some food. Are you okay? Has anything else happened? Have the police let you know if they've got them?'

I shake my head. 'You just get home. We can order food in. And no, I haven't heard anything. But Prim visited.'

'Really?' His voice rises in surprise. 'What did she want? Is she still there?'

'No, she's gone. Patrick, I told Prim about the baby. She wasn't happy. Not at all.'

'You did a test already? You're pregnant?' I can't tell if the shock in his voice is positive or not.

'No, but I think I am.'

'Okay, but you shouldn't get your hopes up. Not until you've done a test.'

He's right. I shouldn't. But I don't want to talk about the baby now, anyway. I want to go back to Prim.

'Patrick, Prim said something to me. Something strange. Did you give Arabella an eternity ring two weeks before you left her?' There's silence at the end of the line. It's all I need to confirm it. 'Why? Why would you do that? Why would you give someone a gift like that? Is it because you knew we were just going to be a fling and you'd go back to her in the end?'

'What? No!' This time there's no delay in his answer. 'Did Prim say that? It wasn't like that at all. It wasn't. I don't know. I guess my head was in a mess.'

His answer doesn't do much for my confidence. 'You said that when you were with me, your head was the clearest it had ever been. That you had no doubt at all that we were meant to be together.' I know exactly how desperate I sound, but I can't help it. That damn phone call I overheard, and then Prim, not to mention the bloody fire. My head is everywhere. 'You said things with her were awful. Why would you give someone an eternity ring if you were going to leave? And why does Prim think that everything between you was absolutely perfect?'

'Well, Prim wasn't there, you know that. When we got together, she was already off flunking university. She wants to believe whatever she wants to believe.'

'But the ring. She didn't make that part up.'

'No, she didn't. But it's not like she thought. That ring was my mother's. That's why I gave it to her.'

God, it hits even worse than before. I want to throw up. 'You gave her your mother's eternity ring?' Surely that's even worse than just buying one.

'My mother and Arabella got on well. Really well. She always said that she couldn't wait to see her rings on Arabella's hand. And she did, with her engagement ring and her wedding ring, too. But when it came to the eternity ring... I'd never given it to Arabella because things were always so messy. I guess I didn't want to make her think everything was okay. Then I was packing up my things, ready to move in with you. Ready to say goodbye, and that's when I saw it. It wasn't about what Arabella wanted, it was about my mother. That ring was about her. That was why I needed Arabella to have it. You know better than anyone that things don't always make sense when it comes to grief?'

I don't think it's a question he expects me to answer. Patrick is one of the few people who knows exactly what happened when my mother died, but that doesn't mean we talk about it. In my silence, he carries on.

'When I found it there, I felt like she'd be so disappointed in me. You know, that I'd fallen in love with someone else. I was leaving the woman I said I was going to spend the rest of my life with, who she had loved like a daughter. I needed to do something to show her I hadn't just forgotten everything she said. Does that make sense? It probably doesn't. I understand why you'd think it was strange, but—'

'I get it,' I say, interrupting him. 'Of course I get it. Let's be honest, when it comes to doing strange things because of your mother, I'm hardly one to talk, am I?'

He doesn't reply, but somehow, even on a phone call, I can see the expression on his lips. The mix of guilt and pain from having to relieve his past wounds, not to mention making me go through mine.

'Do you forgive me?' he says. 'Maybe I should have told you, but I didn't think about it. I really didn't. It was more a goodbye gift than anything else.'

'Did Arabella see it that way?'

For the first time since Patrick and I started our relationship, I feel a flicker of sadness for his ex-wife. She was a bitch, sure. Completely undeserving of him. But to get a gift like that, then have your husband leave only days later, must have stung like hell.

'I think she knew, yes. Look, I'll talk to you about it when I get home if you still want to? Also, maybe you should do the pregnancy test when I get back too. It might be too soon, but you never know?'

'Maybe,' I say.

'Okay, see you soon. Love you.'

When I hang up, my mind is almost as muddled as it was before. I'm relieved that he's coming home, that's for sure, and he didn't deny the eternity ring. That has to mean something too. But I'm still going to have to confront him about the telephone call. About the deleted phone call list. The question is, do I do it before or after the pregnancy test?

44

'Imogen?' His voice bellows into the house a heartbeat after I hear the back door open. 'Where are you?'

'Upstairs. In the bedroom,' I call back.

I'm sitting on the edge of the bed and the test is in my hand. I had to do it. I know I told Patrick I would wait until he got home, but I needed to have the answers before I confronted him about what I heard on the phone. Now I have them.

'Hey, you,' he says as he sweeps into the room. 'I saw the workshop. Thank god you're okay. What are you—' He stops three feet away from me, his eyes wide and mouth open. 'You did it?'

My chin dips in a nod. 'I'm sorry. I just—'

'You don't have to apologise. Is it... are you?' He edges towards me, as if he's scared of the piece of plastic in my hand and its window of hope or heartbreak. My gaze moves back down to that little window. I haven't been able to keep my eyes off it for the last ten minutes, but now it's his turn to see. Swallowing the lump in my throat, I press my lips together and hand the test to Patrick.

For the longest of seconds, there's nothing but silence. Then Patrick's whoop of delight shoots into the night as he sweeps me up in his arms.

'I'm pregnant?' The words come out more as a question than a statement. 'I'm pregnant.'

'You're pregnant!' He grins, before coving his mouth in disbelief. 'You're having a baby! We're having a baby!'

As he plants his lips on mine, I can feel all the joy emanating from him. Any doubt I had that Patrick doesn't want this – doesn't want me – is gone. You can't fake that kind of emotion. It's not possible.

When he finally breaks away, his eyes are glazed with tears. 'It's going to change you, you know. Being a parent is going to change you in ways you've never dreamed of. You'll see. You suddenly have this entirely new person in your life that you will do anything for. Anything to protect them. It's insane.'

'I can feel it already,' I say, placing my hands on my stomach. 'That's silly, isn't it? I shouldn't do that. I shouldn't get attached already. Is it wrong that I feel connected to it so early?'

'Of course it's not. You've made a human. You have a human growing in you. This is the best news. It's just the best news. Everything is falling into place. Just wait and see.'

He kisses me again, with my hands still trapped there against my stomach. Is what he said true? Will I do anything for this small, new human that we've created together? I want to believe it's true. I wouldn't have gone down this route if I thought I wouldn't. But it's hard to ignore my past.

As we break away, Patrick locks his eyes on mine and my smile falters. 'I know what you're thinking,' he says. 'I know why you're worried, but you don't need to be. You're not your mother. You could never be her. And you will never do what she did. I would bet my life on it.'

I press my lips together and draw in a long breath. He's right. I'm not. I know I'm not. I'm already at the age she was when she started going downhill, and apart from that one incident, I've been good. Besides, that incident was different. I had a reason to act that way. Trauma had caused it. All the doctors said as much.

'Come on,' Patrick says, pulling my arm so that I lift my head to look at him. 'This is a special night for you. A really special night. We are going out for dinner to celebrate.'

Instinctively, I turn my head to look out the window. It's too dark to see anything out there, but it doesn't change the smoke on my studio or the trauma I had to go through today.

'I'm not sure. Maybe we shouldn't be leaving the house already.'

'It's fine. Didn't Donny say he was looking into it? Come on. You're not going to have many nights left when you can go out and celebrate whenever you want. I'll jump in the shower, get changed, then we'll be good to go.'

I don't want to head out. I want to talk to him. Talk through my fears, but also my hopes. Talk through that damn conversation I heard him having. But he looks so excited, and it's not just a special night for me, it's a special night for him too, and it's clear this is what he wants to do.

'Okay, that sounds nice.'

His grin widens. 'Why don't you look up the best restaurants in town? No expense spared. Whatever you want.'

Sushi is always my go to but that's out now, though even if it wasn't, I'm not sure I could stomach it. I'm not sure what I can stomach, actually. But if we go somewhere like an Italian restaurant, I'm sure there will be plenty of neutral-tasting foods that won't turn my stomach. I'll just have to check to see exactly what I can eat first.

As Patrick disappears into the shower, I grab my phone,

ready to look up local restaurants only to see a message has come through. There's no name on it and I can tell from the icon that there's a photo attached. My heart leaps. It has to be from Donny. Maybe a photo of the Springfield lads under arrest. Something to do with the case, at least. But when I open it, I find myself staring at the picture of a ring.

The photograph is angled so that I can read the inscription on the inside. I know immediately what I'm looking at. It's Patrick's wedding ring. But the message isn't from Patrick. My hand trembles as I read the words. *If they're still over, then why was this at Mum's house today?*

45

All the blood drains from my face as I read the message over and over. I don't need any name to know who it's from. Prim. She's sent me a photo of Patrick's wedding ring.

A second later, the next message pings through. It's a photo of a bedroom. A luxurious bedroom, with a king-sized bed and silk sheets that are made but slightly rumpled. On the bedside table are two glasses of champagne and a circle has been drawn near the base of one of them. My throat constricts as I zoom in on the area, although I already know what it's showing me – the position of the ring.

'She's just playing with you, Imogen,' I mutter, trying to shake the tightness from my body. She probably just took one of our wedding photos and photoshopped it to make it look like it was in Arabella's bedroom. After all, the wedding photographer took photos of the inscription on the rings. I didn't think Prim had seen them, but maybe Patrick showed her. Yes, that would make sense. He would want his daughter to see his wedding photos, wouldn't he? I try to swallow, but my throat is bone dry and blocked by a lump that refuses to budge. She's just acting out because of earlier in the day, I tell myself, trying to add logic to the situation. She just needs to fight back. To feel like she still has some power. There's no way Patrick would go back to Arabella. Especially not now.

With the phone firmly in my grasp, I stand up and stride over to the ensuite, where I swing the door open. The room is filled with steam from Patrick's shower.

'Hey? Were you going to join me?' he says, grinning. 'There's not a lot of room in here. We might have to put in a larger one.'

'Where's your wedding ring?' I ask, ignoring what he's just said. 'You weren't wearing it earlier when we were looking at the test.'

I don't know if that's true or not. If it's a lie, he'll show me, and I'll know for certain that Prim was just trying to get a rise out of me. If it's not... well, that's a different matter entirely.

Patrick turns the water off, steps out of the shower and wraps a towel around himself. As I glance down, I see the truth. His hand is empty.

'Where is it?' I say.

He shakes his head and groans. 'Shit. I forgot to put it back on.'

'Why did you take it off?' I ask, surprised at how casual he is.

'The photocopier at work's playing up. We couldn't get an engineer out to look at it, so I gave it a go. I didn't want the ring to get caught on something. You know, you hear all these horror stories, don't you? Anyway, I couldn't fix it, but I tried.'

'Don't you have other people in the office who could do something like that?' My heart is racing, but my voice is steady. I'm not letting him brush me off with this. 'Fixing a photocopier doesn't sound like something one of the partners at the firm would do.'

'It was the photocopier in my office,' he says.

'Really?'

'Yeah, my personal one.' The way he stands there so at ease, looking me in the eye, is enough to make my blood boil.

'You're lying to me,' I whisper.

'Im, I swear—'

'Don't lie to me!'

I've never screamed at Patrick before. Not in the two years I've known him. I'm not the type of person who screams, ever. I'm the type who withdraws into herself. Who shrinks so far away from a situation they become near invisible. But I'm not having him stand there and barefaced lie to me. Not when I've just discovered I'm carrying his child. I pull out my phone and hold it out to him. 'Your ring. Next to Arabella's bed.'

'What the...? Where did you get that?' He answers his own question before I can. 'Prim? Did Prim send this to you?' He tries to take the phone from me, but I pull my hand back, stopping him from grabbing it.

'Were you there today? Were you at Arabella's? Is she the one you told you would love forever on the phone last night?'

'You heard—' He stops himself, but it's too late.

'I heard, Patrick. I heard what you said.' Tears tumble down my cheeks, but I make no attempt to wipe them away. 'Why, Patrick? Why?'

He chews on his bottom lip and his eyes flicker down to his feet as water runs down them and forms a puddle on the bathroom floor. My heart feels as though a thousand needles have been pushed into the centre of it. I already know what he's going to say.

'You need to let me explain, Im,' he says quietly. 'It's not what you think.'

46

It's not what you think.

His words echo around in my head as we stand there in the bathroom, goosebumps rising on Patrick's uncovered torso. *It's not what you think.* When have those words ever preceded something you want to hear? *It's not what you think – it was a one-time thing. It's not what you think – it didn't mean anything. It's not what you think.*

But it is, isn't it? There's only one way of looking at this, and it's clear exactly what's happening.

I'm having a baby with Patrick, and he's having an affair with his ex-wife. His controlling, manipulative, unstable wife. The thought is enough to make my adrenaline surge. My breathing becomes shallow and an icy chill spreads over my skin, but I force myself to inhale and stay in the moment. I'm not going to break over this. This isn't when I collapse into a panic attack. He doesn't deserve that. He doesn't deserve anything. I, on the other hand, deserve answers and I'm going to get them.

'How long's it been going on?'

'It's not—'

'Don't you dare say that to me again!' I hiss. 'You took your wedding ring off at your ex-wife's house. And put it on her bedside table, next to two champagne glasses. I'd say it's exactly what I think. And I'm right, aren't I, about the phone call? When you said you'd always love her, you were talking to Arabella, weren't you?'

His expression says it all.

'Fucking hell!' I shake my head.

What the hell has happened? How has my life gone to shit in a matter of days? Last week, I was moving to the countryside with my husband who I adored and trusted completely, ready to start this new chapter of my life. Now, my agent doesn't want to work with me. I'm being terrorised by a bunch of locals I've never even met and I'm having a baby with a man I clearly know nothing about. Everything I thought I knew is falling apart.

'I'm leaving,' I say. I don't know where I'm going, and I don't even care. I just want out. Away from Patrick and away from this fucking house.

I turn around, ready to leave, when he grabs me by the hand. 'It's really not what you think,' he says, spinning me around to face him.

'Get your hands off me,' I growl. 'Get your hands off me now.'

He looks down, and his brow crinkles, as if he's surprised to find himself holding me. But while he loosens his grip, he doesn't let go of me entirely. 'Please, you need to let me explain.'

'You mean wheedle your way out of it?'

'No! I don't. I mean explain. You're right, I *was* talking to Arabella on the phone last night and I *did* tell her that I would love her forever, and maybe that was wrong, because I didn't mean it – not in the way you think I did. But I needed to say it to her. Just like I needed to see her today. Not because I want to be with her, though, but because she's dying, Imogen. Arabella is dying.'

47

Patrick stares at me with tears glazing his eyes. His voice grows quieter as he continues to repeat himself. 'She's dying,' he says again. 'Arabella is dying.'

I stand there, unsure what to do, when he edges towards me. I still don't move, even as he drops his head onto my shoulder and begins to cry.

We stay there together – me unsure if I should move, Patrick sobbing on my shirt – and let time pass around us. Guilt roils through me. How could I have doubted him? This is the man who broke his daughter's heart for me. Who dealt with sniggering behind his back when he became the clichéd older man who had fallen for a younger woman. This is the person who has been with me to every doctor's appointment, regardless of his own commitments, while we tried to build a family of our own. And I doubted him. I doubted him when he was only trying to do the right thing. That's all he ever tries to do, and I've always known that about him. It's the thing I love most about him, for crying out loud. But the one time I actually had to trust him and put my faith in him, without faltering, I couldn't do it.

At some point, his tears stop and he straightens up, wipes his eyes, and looks at me. 'I'm sorry. I know I shouldn't feel like this. I shouldn't. It's ridiculous being this upset, after everything she did to me, but she's Prim's mother. She's my daughter's mother, and she's dying. When I think of how much this is going to break Prim, I… I…' His voice cracks again.

'I'm sorry,' I say. The words don't feel right, but they're the only ones I can think to say. Though there's another question I need to ask. One that, judging from my surprise visit today, I already know the answer to. 'Does Prim know?'

'No.' He shakes his head. 'Arabella's not told many people. I think it's just one other person who knows besides me. A friend who's been going to appointments with her. She doesn't want Prim to know, though. We've had a hard enough time keeping that girl on the rails as it is. I think this would be the final straw.'

I've never seen him look so grey. So tired. So defeated. I want to believe him, 100 per cent. And I do. I believe Arabella is sick, and that's why he told her he loved her. But there's still one thing that's causing my stomach to churn with such ferocity it's making me nauseous. After all, if Patrick was willing to tell Arabella he still loved her, because he knew it was what she needed to hear, what else would he be willing to do? The thought alone is enough to make me feel sick, and I don't want to entertain it, but I have to know for sure.

'You took your wedding ring off in her bedroom. There were champagne glasses there. Why? That doesn't make sense to me, Patrick. If all you were doing was supporting her, why would you do that?'

He nods solemnly. 'She was drinking in her bedroom when I got there. Well, drunk more like. She knew I was coming. I'd promised her I would when we spoke last night and so she'd opened a bottle of bubbles and wanted us to have a toast to our lives together.' He looks like he's about to carry on, but instead, he digs his hands into his hair as he shakes his head. When he looks back at me, his eyes are red with burgeoning tears. 'I get how screwed up this all is, Im. I swear I do. But I didn't do anything with her. I promise on your life. On this baby's life. The sight of my wedding ring upset her. Maybe I shouldn't have taken it off, maybe I should have been firmer with her, but I was worried. Worried about her doing something, so I took it off. I just forgot about it. I promise that's what happened. I would never do anything to hurt you like that. You know I love you. You know I do. But Arabella – she's still my family. She's Prim's mum so she always will be, and you know I'll do anything for my family.'

I blow out a lungful of air in a sigh. 'Do you have any idea of time?' I ask. 'How long she's got left?'

He shakes his head. 'She said she's known she's been sick for months, but the doctors told her it was a long shot of recovery.' He scoffs bitterly. 'That basically gave her permission to give up, in her head at least. Rather than having treatment, she's just pretending nothing's wrong. Travelling, drinking. She's taken up smoking again. She's an absolute wreck.'

'When did you find out?' I ask.

'Last night. That was the first I knew of it, and I was going to tell you tonight. I promise. I was going to. But then you rang me about the fire, and then you're pregnant, and it's amazing, but shit, there's a lot going on right now. So I'm sorry, I'm sorry I left my ring there, and I'm sorry I didn't tell you the truth about what happened last night. But I promise, I am with you in this. One hundred per cent. Okay? It's you and me. Always.'

His hands are squeezing mine so tightly, my knuckles are pressed together, but I don't tell him to let go. He needs that. He needs the reassurance of me being there for him. I can feel that now, more than ever. 'What are you going to do? When are you going to tell Prim?' I ask.

He shakes his head. 'It's not up to me. I would tell her now, you know, so the pair of them have a chance to say a proper goodbye. But Arabella doesn't want that, and I can't go against her wishes. Not now.'

'I understand,' I say, before adding the other words I owe him. 'And I'm sorry. I'm sorry I didn't trust you.'

He nods and allows a small smile to creep onto his lips.

'So, that wasn't quite the celebration I had planned for tonight.' He laughs. 'What do you want to do now? Stay in? Go out? It's your choice. Whatever you need I'm here for you. I'll always be here for you. You know that, right?'

I nod. 'We'll always be here for each other,' I say.

48

We don't go out to celebrate my pregnancy the way we'd planned. Instead, Patrick orders some takeaway, and we talk. Occasionally about the baby, but most of the time, Prim and Arabella dominate the conversation – more so even than the fire at the studio. You know something serious is happening when it overshadows a near-death experience. But my experience was just that – *near* death. Arabella, on the other hand, has been given her death sentence.

'Doesn't she want to fight?' I say. 'For Prim's sake, if not hers?'

He shakes his head. 'She said she's scared of losing herself in the treatment. You know, turning into some frail old woman.'

'But if it gets her a few more months?'

'I think, in her head, a few more months of struggling, needing people, feeling weak... it isn't worth it for her. I know it's terrible timing for us with the baby, but I think I'm going to need to be there for her. Some of the time, at least.'

There's only one answer I can give, and surprisingly, it's the one I want to offer. I want to give Patrick all the support he needs.

'I get it. Really, I do. Was that where you were going to spend tonight?'

'I was going to go into the office. Catch up on the work I really need to do. But I thought maybe having me there in the evening would convince her to tell Prim.' He snorts slightly. 'God, saying it like that makes it sound like I was going to emotionally blackmail her—'

'It doesn't at all,' I assure him. 'I completely get where you're coming from. And I'm so sorry. I'm so sorry you have to deal with this.'

'Arabella's dealt with some pretty tough things in the past. We'll deal with this,' he says.

I nod and wonder, not for the first time, if he's talking about something specific. He often mentions how he and Arabella survived some 'shitstorm', but the way he speaks about it always gives me the impression he wants to leave it in the past. And I get that. I get having a history you don't like talking about. And there's no point being jealous of whatever shared moments he and his ex-wife have. Whatever they were, the bonds they formed weren't strong enough to keep him and me apart.

'I was going to go back tomorrow,' he says, breaking my thoughts. 'After work. But I get it if you have a problem with that. And I won't be home late.'

'I—'

'You could always come to work with me,' he says before I can get a word out. 'You know, if you're worried about being here on your own. But I really don't feel like you have to be. I saw a couple of police cars not too far up on the road. They're obviously doing a patrol around here to make sure nothing else happens. I'm sure now that the kids have got the pranks out of their systems, they'll be done. Which reminds me, I've ordered a security camera system. It should come the day after tomorrow. I'll set it up as soon as it arrives.'

'Thank you. And I'll be okay. I want to sort out the mess in the studio. See how bad the damage is. I think it's okay, but I'll probably work in the house instead. And I thought I might ask Maureen if she wanted to come over, too. You know, a bit of safety in numbers.'

'That sounds like a good idea. And from now on, I will tell you every time I'm visiting her. No hiding things, okay?'

'And no nights in London?' I ask. As comforting as it is to know the police are taking this seriously, I don't really want to spend the night on my own.

'I will be home every evening. I promise you.' He kisses me before he places a hand on my stomach. 'Trust me, everything's going to work out just fine. I can feel it.'

49

The next morning, Patrick and I leave the house at the same time. Him to go to work, me to go to the shops.

'If you need me, call me. You two are still my priority. You know that, right?'

'Of course I do.' It sounds unconvincing, even to myself.

He arches his eyebrows.

'I do,' I say. 'It's fine. I guess it's just not quite the pregnancy I expected.'

'Oh, wait until they're born. Nothing about having a newborn's expected.' He laughs, but I can't reciprocate it.

'I'm not sure if that's meant to make me feel better or not.'

With his smile still in place, he kisses me on the lips. 'It'll be amazing. I promise you. And remember to check what you're allowed to eat. I'm sure you'll find a list somewhere online.'

'Don't worry, I've already got one.'

At the supermarket, I park in the first spot I see and climb out of the car, yet I've barely shut the door when someone starts yelling. 'What are you doing there? Yes, I'm talking to you.' I turn around to find a small woman with a pushchair glaring at me. 'You can't park there,' she says. 'It's a parent-and-child space.' She points to the sign on the ground, the painted blue pushchair. 'These spaces are for people who actually need them, you know. Kids, or pregnant people or something.'

My mind had been so full of the pregnancy and impending arrival of our little one that driving into the space had felt like the most natural thing to do. I didn't think how it would be perceived.

'I... I am,' I say, putting my hand against my stomach, though there's absolutely nothing to show for it. After barely eating for the last couple of days, I've probably lost weight rather than gained.

The woman's nose twitches as she glowers at me. 'Bloody waste of space, some people,' she mutters before turning away.

For a second, I consider yelling after her, telling her that I *am* pregnant and therefore should be able to use these parking spaces too. But then again, maybe that's not true. There are people far more pregnant than me, people who can't walk as easily or who need to get children in and out of car seats while juggling bags of shopping, keys and everything else parents have to juggle. I'm sure if I see someone looking like me parking here nine months from now, I'll probably be pissed off, too. Still, I decide to leave the car and head into the shop.

It feels like there are mothers and children everywhere. Everywhere I look is another child in a pushchair. Sometimes they're with their dads or grandparents, but mostly it's mothers with children. As much as I wish the stereotype didn't stick, it does, and it hurts. I'm sure my mother would have taken me to the shops when I was little. I know she had her issues, but I can't believe she was like the neighbour we had who just left her child when they went out for the evening. But maybe she was.

Maybe that was where all my issues started and I'll never even be able to remember it.

When I'm done, I hurry back to my car, just in case the woman is still around.

On the way back home, I find myself feeling unexpectedly low. Pregnancy does that, I get that. It throws all your hormones into whack, but the IVF has already been doing that for months. It's the fact that I don't want to go back to the house that is making me feel this way. I've not heard anything from Donny, and while I'd like to think no news is good news, it's tough to believe that in this situation. After all, if there'd been an arrest, I'm sure he would've let me know.

This isn't how I'm supposed to feel, is it? Nervous about heading home, terrified of what's waiting for me? Wondering if my husband will come home to me or spend the night with his ex-wife? No, I'm not worried about that. Patrick said it as clear as day earlier. I'm his priority, not her, but what about when Prim finds out that the IVF was successful and she needs him too? How's he going to choose between a child that actually needs him and one that isn't even born yet?

As I hit the country lanes, my feelings of melancholy are accompanied by nervousness. How long am I meant to remain nervous of my own home before we admit moving here was a mistake? If we were to sell up now, we'd lose so much money. The legal fees, the estate agent's fees – it would be a financial hit. But I could earn that back easily enough, couldn't I? Another exhibition, an online auction... Sure, Orla doesn't want to deal with me now, but there are plenty of people who would. Besides, I could always just sell online like Patrick and I discussed. But clawing back my sanity? That takes far longer. I know that now.

I park on the lane and open the gate. Last night's rain has

turned the ground to mud, and it'll only get worse over the next month or so. An electric gate has now made it to the top of my priority list, along with the security system. Fingers crossed that arrives tomorrow.

I feel a sense of unexpected relief when I find the door still locked. Half of me had expected it to be open again, with Prim waiting inside. Or the Springfield kids. Or whoever it was *watching* me from the field. My hands sting from the weight of the bags. I know I'm not going to make it all the way to the kitchen. The handles are digging into my palms so hard it feels like they're going to break the skin.

I drop the bags at the entrance and take just one through into the kitchen. But I don't get any further than the doorway. I freeze. Someone has been in the house and they've left a message for me. A message that causes my blood to run cold.

50

I'm not even sure how I'm still standing. My knees have lost all their strength and I can feel them trembling, desperate to drop me to the ground, but somehow I inch forward. My eyes remain locked on the object in front of me as it sits on the kitchen table. There's no mistaking what it is: a funeral wreath. White flowers, arranged perfectly to spell out a name. *My* name.

An involuntary gag has me choking back my breath, but I keep on walking until I'm standing right next to it. There's not a yellowing or browning petal in sight. Just dozens upon dozens of pristine white blooms. While I've seen plenty of these in my life – in florists, or passing funeral processions in the car – I've only ever been close enough to touch one before. My mother's. The difference between that one and this one is that my mother was actually dead. This is just a threat. A very clear one.

I draw in a long breath, trying to keep my mind steady. I need to stay here in the moment. At least I know now that this wasn't some prank. Whoever set fire to my studio – whether it was the Springfield kids or not – they weren't expecting me to get out. That was never their plan. Their plan was for me to die in there. And this wreath confirms that.

With my eyes still fixed on the flowers, I move around the table. I keep a wide berth, like it might jump off the table and fly towards me. I didn't know it was possible to be so scared of inanimate objects, but at this moment, that's exactly how I feel.

I'm not sure what I'm looking for exactly. A card perhaps. A handwritten note with an identifiable script that the police could use to ID my tormentor. Or just the name of the florist, so I can track them down. But what I find is a thousand times worse.

My hands fly to my mouth as I try to stifle my gasp, but it doesn't stop the tears from tumbling down my cheeks. They didn't just break into my house and leave a wreath with my name on it. There's a second flower arrangement too, and though I wouldn't have thought it possible, it's even more sinister. Dozens of flowers have been packed closely together to form the shape of a teddy bear. I don't need to have attended many funerals to know this is the type of tribute that would be made for a child who's died Whoever this is, they want my baby dead, too. This has gone too far. Way too far.

I grab my phone from my pocket and dial Patrick's number on video call. I'm terrified he's going to be with Arabella or in a meeting, but I'm prepared to ring a hundred times if that's what it takes to get through to him.

Thankfully, he answers straight away. But rather than seeing his face, I get a fuzzy image, like old TV static.

'Hey, is everything okay?' he asks.

'No, no, it's not.' I spin the camera around to show him. 'This was in the house.'

'Are you on video? I can't see – I've just walked into the underground. What are you showing me?'

I feel sick. 'It's a wreath, Patrick.'

'For the door? That sounds nice.'

'No, not for the fucking door! It's a memorial wreath. The kind you give someone when they're dead, and it's got my name on it!'

'What?' I wish I could see his face, but the signal is so bad the picture just keeps flickering, then turning black on the screen. 'What do you mean?'

'I mean, someone came into the house and did this! They're threatening me, Patrick! They're threatening me. And there's a teddy bear too. Teddy bears are for *children*, Patrick. They're threatening the baby too!'

Silence meets my response. No questions. Nothing. 'I'm on my way to see Arabella,' he says eventually. 'She was seriously upset when she rang me this morning. I think Prim has found out.'

My stomach clenches, turning my insides into a mass of knots. 'Patrick, I need you here!'

'I know. I was about to say I would turn around, okay? I won't go and see her. I'll get off at the next station and turn around. That's what I'll do. I won't be long. Promise. I'll get straight on the train and come home, okay? But don't wait in the house. And leave it where it is, all right? Leave the wreaths where they are. Don't touch them. The police will want to take photos. Make sure it stays exactly where it is. You haven't touched it, have you?'

I shake my head before remembering he can't see me. 'No, I haven't.'

'Good. Well, leave it where it is and get out of the house. Go to Maureen's.'

'What if she's not there?' I say, envisioning the worst-case scenario. What if she's not there and whoever did this is still here, listening in to the conversation?

'If she's not in, wait on her doorstep and ring me back. I'll stay on the line until she comes home, okay?'

I nod. 'Okay.'

'I'll come and get you from Maureen's. Stay out of the house until we know what's going on. I'll be as fast as I can. I promise. I love you, Im. We'll figure out who's doing this, I promise. They won't get away with this.'

'I love you too,' I say. 'Please, hurry up.'

'I'm coming. I'm coming now,' he says. A second later, his phone cuts out.

51

As I put my phone down on the table, I wipe away the tears streaming down my face. This isn't the type of stunt a load of bored teenagers would do. This type of thing takes planning. They would have needed to order the wreath days ago, watched the house to make sure we weren't in, not to mention spent money on getting it made.

This has been thought out.

I don't even bother unpacking the shopping. I know there's frozen stuff in there, but I don't care. Food can be replaced – this baby and I can't. I don't touch the flowers either. Patrick's right. I need to leave them exactly where they are for when the police come to look at them. And honestly, I don't *want* to touch them. I wouldn't put it past whoever did this to cover them in something that could trigger an allergic reaction if I tried to pick them up.

As I leave, I slam the door behind me and check it's locked when a thought strikes me. Whoever this was, they got into the house without breaking anything, which means either they're great at picking locks or they have a key.

A tightness forms in my throat as I head back inside. When Prim gave me the key back, I didn't bother checking it closely. I was just so grateful she was going. I put it on the shelf and forgot about it. But what if she knew that was what I'd do?

It takes only a minute to find the key. My heart twists in my chest because I already know what I'm about to see. But just to be sure, I take my own keychain, separate them out until I find the one I want and lay them side by side.

They're both brass Yale keys, but that's where the similarities end. The shaft of mine is at least half a centimetre longer, and the grooves are far more detailed. There's no chance they open the same lock. Whatever key Prim gave to me, it wasn't the one to our front door. Which means she still has her copy. Which means she could still get into the house.

'Fuck!' I scream. I should have known all along. It was my first instinct to believe she was the one who had set fire to the shed and now I've got the evidence to prove it. I don't care how devastated she's going to be about Arabella's diagnosis, she can be devastated from a prison cell.

I try calling Patrick again, but the call goes straight to voicemail. I suspect he's ringing Arabella, telling her he won't be able to come over, but it doesn't matter. The evidence will still be here for him to see when he gets back.

The knowledge brings a small sense of relief, but I'm still not keen to stay in the house. So after deciding I'm not going to let Prim be responsible for good food going off, I put everything away, then take Patrick's advice and head over to Maureen's.

52

It's more squashed fly biscuits and tea at Maureen's, but honestly, I don't mind. There's something about the dryness of the biscuits that helps ease my morning sickness, and I'm getting used to the overly sweet tea, too.

'I'm sorry, love,' Maureen says, looking worried. 'I've not heard of the Springfield lot doing anything like this. To be honest, they were always the physical prank type of lads – you know, breaking windows, moving things about.' She shakes her head and smacks her lips together. 'No, it doesn't sound like them. But then again, they're older now.'

'I think it was Prim,' I say, my voice lower than I expect.

'Prim?' Maureen's brow furrows.

'Patrick's daughter.'

Her frown deepens. 'Why's that? Do you and her not get on, then?'

I don't even try to hide my disdain. 'No, we don't. She turned up at the house yesterday, threatening my baby. She's also the only person who has a key. I thought she gave it back to me, but she didn't. She tricked me. Gave me another one. Why would she do that unless she was planning something? Besides, she's the only person who knows about the pregnancy.'

At this, Maureen purses her lips.

'Well, I can't disagree with the other bits, but that's not strictly true about the baby part.'

'What do you mean? Prim's the only person I've told. Other than you, that is. I didn't want to tell her. It wasn't out of spite or anything, but she pushed me and I was worried she was going to hurt the baby. So I told her.'

'But she's not the only person who knows,' Maureen says. 'Remember how you were shouting it when you were locked in that shed of yours? That's when I heard. I'm sure the Springfield lads heard too, if it was them. Anyone close enough would have. And I'm sure there are other people who've noticed too. Sounds silly, but people pick up on these things. People you know. Like you not having a drink around mine. Friends would have spotted it when you act differently. Someone might have seen you buy the pregnancy tests. There are lots of different people who might have cottoned on without you noticing.'

My mind flicks to the man lurking in the shadows on my first night here. Could he have heard me crying out? If loitering around here is one of *his pastimes* then I guess so. My stomach knots tighter as I think about Donny. He knows too, and while Maureen trusts him explicitly, it wouldn't be the first time a cop had done something less than legal. But it doesn't change the fact that only Prim had the key to the house.

'I'm absolutely positive it's her,' I say, possibly to convince myself as much as Maureen.

'Well, you know her better than I do, and someone's obviously doing something. You can't think of anyone else who would have something against you?'

'Against me? No.' I'm the type of person who avoids conflict at all costs. There's no way I would have done something to warrant this without knowing.

'No enemies? Competitors? No one who would profit from you suffering like this.'

It's the word 'profit' that causes a spark in my mind. Orla has been begging me to paint a darker collection again. She wants those emotionally laden, deep paintings I did after my mother died. But I haven't done that style since before I got with Patrick. What better way to push me back into that state than by making me feel like I'm slipping into madness?

She knew we were doing IVF too, and from the way I was reluctant to lift the heavy objects, she could have put two and two together. And then if I add in the hairdryer... she was the one who put them all away. She would have had plenty of time to change the fuse and put in the wrong one while I was cleaning the outside windows. She could have even taken an imprint of my key to get another one made. She certainly has the ability to do that. Either that or... Fuck. They met each other. Of course they did. They met at the wedding. A wedding where they both felt like they were losing something. My hand shakes so much that tea spills over the top of my mug.

'They're working together,' I say, my voice cracking as the words escape. 'Orla and Prim are doing this together.'

53

'Orla? Who's that then?'

My body flinches as Maureen's voice brings me back to the moment.

'Orla,' I say, forcing her name from my throat more clearly this time. 'She's... she's someone I used to work with.'

'Is that right? Then maybe we should ring Donny. Give him a name to work with?'

I shake my head. Maureen is obviously fond of Donny, and maybe he's good enough at dealing with whatever plainclothes cases he gets given at work, but the fact is, this incident has happened less than twenty-four hours after my studio was set on fire. I know Patrick had said he'd seen a police car on the road last night, but if they'd had more of a presence then Orla might not have felt bold enough to keep terrorising me. I can't help thinking that he should have had someone call me for a more formal interview by now, too. Things in the countryside move differently, I get that. But surely attempted murder is attempted murder wherever you are?

'Patrick said to wait for him to get back and then he'll ring the police,' I say. 'I know it'll probably take longer than dealing with Donny directly, but I think if we go through as many channels as possible, they might finally take notice.'

Maureen nods. 'You need to do what's best for you,' she says.

'Yes. You're right. You're right.'

I place my mug of tea down on the side table and stand up.

'Sorry, Maureen. I'll just be a second. I need to make a phone call.'

'Oh, no problem. I'll put on the kettle. Make sure you've got a fresh brew when you're done.'

I get that by moving into the kitchen, Maureen is trying to give me the privacy to make the phone call in here, but I know how thin these walls are, and this isn't a conversation I want overheard, and so I grab my coat and head outside.

I don't bother second-guessing myself as I scroll down the names in my phone and hit call on Orla's name.

'Im,' she says brightly. 'This is a nice surprise. I wasn't expecting to hear from you.'

'No, I'm sure you weren't.' There's no point in bothering with niceties. She's lost the right to those. 'Did you not think I'd figure it out?'

'Figure out what? Sorry, I'm confused.'

I scoff. It's actually amusing listening to her try to act like she's all innocent. 'This stops, Orla. I'd expect it of Prim. I've always known what a bitch she is, but you were supposed to be my friend.'

'Prim? What's she done now?'

'I know it's you and the police are going to know, too. The minute Patrick comes home, we're going to the police and you are going to pay for this.'

'Imogen, what are you talking about?'

'You can pretend all you like, but I know and I won't let you get away with it. It won't work. Your games won't work. Do you understand?'

'Imogen, I—' Her voice stutters on the other end of the line. Stuttering – surely that's a sign someone's lying.

'Just so you know, if I ever do go back to that style of painting, which I won't, you can be sure as hell that you won't be representing me. I can't believe I actually thought you were my friend.'

'Please, Im, you're not making any sense.' I can hear the false desperation in her voice. 'I'm worried. Are you okay?'

This time my laugh fully forms. 'I should start worrying about yourself,' I say. 'The police will be there soon.'

With that, I hang up.

54

The smile that rises on my lips feels like freedom. It's done. These last three days of horror are over. Orla is an intelligent woman. There's no way she'd risk doing something now that she knows we're onto her. I just have to hope that I was right in believing the police will be able to collect enough evidence to put her behind bars. The thought jolts through me. Orla behind bars. It's not something I could have ever perceived, let alone dreamt I would want, and yet this is what she's pushed me to.

With a weight lifted from my shoulders, I go back into Maureen's house to find her slipping into her thick wax jacket.

'Everything okay, dear?' she asks.

'I think so. Yes, it is,' I add with a little more certainty. 'I think I might have got to the bottom of it. I think it might all be over now.'

'Well, that's very good news. Now, you're welcome to stay here as long as you like, but I was going to take Brutus for a walk. It'd be nice to have some company, if you're up for it. Maybe you might even find a view or two you want to paint?'

'That sounds good. A walk sounds good,' I say. The speed at

which I answer surprises me, but the smile that rises on her lips only makes me surer I've made the right decision. Maybe Patrick wasn't completely off the mark with his Auntie Maureen remark, after all. She's certainly been more support to me than any member of my biological family ever was.

'Perfect,' she says. 'Let me grab his lead and we'll get going.'

The bleakness of the day does little to erase the beauty of the countryside. There's boldness in the greens that fight against the fading light, elegance in the branches that stand in stark silhouettes against the blanket of the sky.

'Now, where are we going to go here, Brutus?' Maureen says as we reach a fork in the path. 'I can never remember which way is better. One's a short loop, the other's much longer. Now which is which?'

'I thought you'd done these hundreds of times,' I say, surprised by her confusion.

'Sorry? Oh yes, I have. It's just the mud, you see. One path stays dry, nice and easy. The other's full of puddles and quagmires. That's what makes it longer, see?' She looks around, then back at me with a broad smile. 'Well, it looks like Brutus has decided for us,' she says, nodding towards the dog, already bounding ahead. 'So this way it is.'

I'm not sure if it's the short or long route we take, but the walk lasts just over an hour and as we approach Cedar Lane, my head actually feels clear. Not only that, but I'm hungry for the first time in days. I feel like I might be able to stomach some food later. Maybe a bowl of pasta and cheese. Nothing exciting, but something to fill me up a bit more. At some point, this unborn child is going to need actual nutrients – nutrients that I haven't been giving them since I found out I was pregnant. I'm even more glad I didn't just dump the frozen food now.

My good mood is made even better when I see the car on the

driveway. I didn't bother ringing Patrick to tell him about Orla. I figured I would fill him in on everything when he got back.

'Well, I guess this is where I leave you?' Maureen says, stopping outside the house. Yet before she can carry on walking, I wrap my arms around her, squeezing the old lady as tightly as I can.

'Thank you, Maureen. Thank you for everything.'

When I let go, she looks pale from shock, and I'm hit with the sudden urge to apologise. After all, you don't know how people feel about physical affection, but before I do, she smiles and nods.

'Any time, Imogen. Any time.'

55

Patrick opens the door before I even reach it, though his eyes don't immediately land on me. Instead, they fall on Maureen, who's still on the lane behind with Brutus, who lets out several loud barks, as if offering a farewell. A moment later, Patrick turns into the house, leaving me to follow him.

'Patrick, I know who's behind it. It's Orla,' I say. 'Orla's been doing all these things, and Prim's been helping her. I think it's so I would go back to my old painting style.'

'Really?' His words come out as a sigh as his back remains facing me.

'That would be why she came down, to make an imprint of my key so she could get one made. I don't think she ever went back to London. I think she's stayed here. If the police can prove it I'm sure that'll be enough to make them look into her.' I wait for him to answer, but there's nothing. Just silence. 'Patrick, is everything okay?' I ask. He hasn't even asked me how I am. 'You seem... off.'

'Where are the flowers, Imogen?' he says.

'The flowers? They were on the kitchen table,' I say. 'In the middle.'

He shakes his head. 'There's nothing here, Imogen. There was nothing here when I came in.'

'What do you mean?' I push past him to look at the table. It's bare. Nothing. No flowers, no wreath. They're gone.

'This doesn't make sense,' I say, feeling a chill run down my spine. 'They were here. I swear to God, Patrick. Orla is doing this to play with me. You know that, don't you?'

I look around frantically. 'I was at Maureen's. We went for a walk. She must've taken them while I was out. Maybe she binned them.' My heart pounds with soaring adrenaline as I turn to leave, but Patrick catches me.

'There's nothing in the bin, Im. That's the first place I checked. I thought maybe you'd moved them after all.'

'Then she took them. Drove off with them. I can prove it. There must be some petals somewhere. There must be.' I try to drop to my knees, to scour the floor for a single white petal to confirm what I saw, but Patrick is holding me firmly so that I can't move. 'Patrick. please. You don't understand. I can prove this to you. I know I can. I can prove it was them. It was Orla and—'

'Imogen, just stop! Don't you think you've done enough?'

'What?'

My face crumples and for the first time since I've got home, I look directly at Patrick. His skin is sallow. His eyes narrow.

'Orla rang me on the way back here, saying she was worried about you. That you were ranting and raving. Saying the police were coming after her?'

'They will! She deserves to go to jail for her part in this. I should never have let her in the house.'

'She's never been here, Imogen!' Patrick's voice bellows

around the kitchen. Just like I'd never shouted at Patrick before the other night, he's never so much as raised his tone to me. Hearing it causes my entire body to recoil.

'What?' I step back, feeling my head shake. 'What are you on about? She was here. You know this. She helped me with the studio, then dumped me as her client.'

He presses his lips tightly together before he lets out a long sigh.

'But that's not true, is it? I spoke to her. When I said about you being upset because she'd dropped you, she didn't know what I was on about. She's been in Edinburgh for the last week.'

'No, that can't be right. She's lying. She's lying to you to throw you off. And she knows that Prim hates me. She knows she would be able to rope Prim into doing this. They're making me look like I'm going crazy.'

Patrick lets out a sharp laugh, but it's not disbelief – it's anger. 'You're really going to bring Prim into this after what *you* did to *her*?'

'What? What do you mean, what *I* did? I haven't done anything to her!'

'The emergency with Arabella today, the reason I had to go see her, was because Prim told her what *you* did to her yesterday.'

'What?' I shake my head, confused, trying to grasp what he's saying. 'What I did? I didn't do anything. She came to the house. She used the key—'

'I know she used the key. The one *I* gave her. And apparently, you thought that was enough of a reason to hit her black and blue.'

'What?' My voice cracks. 'I didn't— What are you talking about? I didn't hit her!'

Patrick pulls out his phone. 'I spoke to her on a video call.

Not that she was in much of a position to speak. I've seen what you did to her.'

I can feel the weight of his stare, his anger, like daggers in my chest. None of this makes sense. The way he looks at me; it's full of disgust, distrust, and absolute repulsion.

'Patrick, I don't understand. I swear I didn't do anything.'

'Maybe the photos will jog your memory,' he says coldly as he hands me his phone. The image on the screen is almost enough to make me gag. It's Prim all right, but it doesn't look like her. Her right eye is swollen shut. Her bottom lip is split and the entire left side of her face mottled in black and blues.

I gasp. 'What happened to her?'

Patrick scoffs. 'You're seriously going to play that card? She told us the way you attacked her.'

'No, no! I didn't! I didn't push her – she *fell*.'

'You didn't push her to get the key from her? And when she landed, her face smacked against the counter? You don't remember that?'

'No! I mean, I was the one who fell against the counter, but I caught myself! And yes, we grappled, but I would've noticed if she'd been hurt, Patrick! You have to believe me. I didn't do this. I would've known if I'd done this.'

As he shakes his head, the blackness in his eyes fades from anger to defeat, while his shoulders slump forward.

'You really believe that, don't you?'

'Yes, of course I do, because it's the truth.'

'Just like Orla coming to visit, and the funeral wreaths on the table.'

'Yes!' I don't know why this is so hard. I've never lied to him, and why the hell would I lie about things like this?

He closes his eyes before he draws a long inhale through his nose. Almost as if he's centring himself for whatever is coming next.

'There are no flowers here, Imogen. Orla has been in Edinburgh, and Prim is hurt. Look, I don't know how else to say this, but these last few days – maybe even before we started the move, with the IVF and all that pressure – it's been too much stress for you. And now there's the hormones from the baby and they're obviously affecting you too. I think this might have been what it was like when your mother died. When you got sick. I think it's happening again, Im.'

56

I still remember the time I told Patrick what happened with my mother. It had been over ten years since the incident, and he was the first person, other than a doctor, who I had told. I trembled as I lay with my head on his chest, trying to still the shaking in my hands and lungs. How torn I felt, knowing that telling him might cause him to flee from my life forever – but needing him to know. If he stayed with me after that, then I knew we would be able to conquer anything. We were meant to be together.

I don't know how long it took me to find the words. How many pauses I needed to regather myself or wipe away the tears. It was different from the therapy sessions. In those, they would always prompt you with questions. Questions like 'How did it make you feel,' or 'What's it like when you remember those days?'

I was forced to make up the answers because therapists expect you to say something, but I wasn't really *thinking* or *feeling* during those days after my mother's death. I don't think there's any word for the numb hollowness with which I roamed the earth. 'Existing' doesn't do it justice.

Did I know what I was doing was crazy? I must have. On some level, I must've known or I wouldn't have tried so hard to hide it. I wouldn't have faked smiles at school. Hell, I wouldn't have even gone to school. So, yes, on some level, I knew my behaviour wasn't natural, but that's not like what's happening now.

'Imogen.' Patrick's voice pulls me out of my memories. 'We need to talk about this. We *have* to talk about this. Maybe… maybe this is like what happened after your mum…'

My head spins around to face him.

'Don't, Patrick, don't do this.'

'But do you think it could be similar? Do you think that maybe the hormones from the baby have brought back the trauma, that you're just seeing things that aren't there? Like when you saw her.'

I shake my head, refusing to accept what he's saying. 'That was different.'

'Why? It was a psychotic break, Imogen. You were seeing things that weren't there. Ignoring reality for your own fabricated world. That's exactly what's happening here.'

'No, it's not!' I scream at him and lift my arms into the air, as if I'm going to punch it, but he grabs me before I can.

'I'm not saying this to make you angry, Imogen. I'm trying to make you see sense.' His eyes are locked on mine. His voice is steady but tense. 'You're telling me there was a floral wreath – a funeral wreath with your name on it – in this house, and now it's gone. You're telling me your agent came to the house, when she's hundreds of miles away, and you don't remember beating my daughter up. Then there were the things with the pins in the tyres. From where I'm standing, it's hard to ignore that.'

'Somebody did that *to me,*' I snap.

He opens his mouth as if he's about to say something, only to close it again. 'You could have opened all the cupboards yourself, Imogen, or changed the fuse in your hairdryer, because no one else had been near it. You have to see this, Imogen. You have to see it from my perspective. Even if I can ignore everything else, even if the... the Springfield kids are behind some of the things, that doesn't change the fact that my daughter is telling me that my wife attacked her.'

'Your daughter is a liar,' I say, my voice shaking. 'You know she lies about things.'

'And I know my wife has had psychotic breaks.' His words hit hard, but he doesn't stop. 'I know you've done things... pretty bad things, and I also know you're under a lot of stress and some of it is my fault. I shouldn't have put so much pressure on you to have a baby. To disrupt your body like that. Then moving here and it not being exactly what we expected. That's going to cause you stress. Surely you can see this is what's happening. Surely you can see there are similarities?'

I shake my head. 'Patrick, please, I can't. I can't do that.' My throat chokes with tears. I can't accept that this could be the same as what happened then, because that would mean having to face up to what happened all those years ago, and that's something I no longer allow myself to do. But maybe I've got no other choice.

57

I found my mother's body in a bathtub filled with water that had turned red. Years later, when I allowed myself to think of it, I wondered if there had been signs. Signs that I – a seventeen-year-old – should have noticed. But every memory of my mother was a sign, and when you see things like that that often, you become immune to it. Immune to the mood swings. To the way she looked at me switching from deep adoration to blunt disgust within a heartbeat.

Some days, she would blame me for where we lived, the state of her life. Even the woman being beaten up upstairs or the neighbours abandoning their kid was, apparently, my fault. Other days, she would sob so loudly it drowned out all the shouting and sirens that filtered in from the outside world. She would pull me close, rock back and forth, and tell me that I was the only reason she kept going. That I was the one good thing in her life.

Like I said, there were always signs. I just didn't think the day would ever actually come.

But this isn't my mother's story, it's mine, and in that

moment, the moment of finding her, something happened to me. My brain refused to accept what it was seeing. It compartmentalised the image, packed it away, and the next day, I went to school like nothing had happened. The entire week, I carried on like normal.

Actually, it was better than normal. The version of Mum that came to me then wasn't the passed-out drunk version I'd grown up with. She wasn't lying on the sofa, vomit down her shirt, while I got ready for school. She was smiling and happy and rather than spending every coin she had on alcohol, she gave me money from her purse to get my packed lunch with.

The next day, when I came home from school, the smell had already started. It wasn't so strong that it had reached my bedroom, but strong enough for me not to want to go into the bathroom. If I had been thinking straight, the fact that my mother's body was lying half submerged in the bathtub should have been the thing that stopped me from going in there. But I wasn't thinking straight. That's why I didn't call the police. That's why I tried to carry on like nothing had happened.

Even now, I can remember the way I pinched my nose as I raced in to get my toothbrush and toothpaste, which I later used at the kitchen sink before going to bed that night. The next morning I treated like any other. I made my sandwiches for school, packed my bag and left, though when I got home, the stench was becoming overpowering. Still I refused to accept what was happening. The flat would often smell bad, particularly when Mum had been on a drinking binge, normally because there was a pile of vomit soaking into the carpet somewhere I hadn't spotted.

On some level, I knew that situation wasn't the same though. That was why I blocked the gap at the bottom of the door with a towel, then burned every incense stick and candle I could find.

Oddly, one of the most distinct memories I have of that time is talking to Mum about it; not the mum who was floating in the bathtub, but the mum my mind created, sitting on the sofa with the television remote in one hand and a glass of wine in the other.

'Do you think it's the drains?' I remember saying to this image of her. 'I bet it's the drains. They played up this time last year, too, don't you remember? Maybe you could ring the house association tomorrow when I'm at school, see if you can get someone to sort it out.'

I can't remember if she replied or not. No, that's not true. I'm sure she did. She'd said something like, 'What did I do to deserve such an amazing, responsible daughter?' or, 'Aren't I lucky to have you looking after everything for us?' Everything she said to me during that time was gentle. Comforting. A million miles away from the woman she'd actually been.

It was her employer that called the police. She hadn't been in for five days, and no one could get hold of her. I don't know why I didn't think about them. Maybe because she'd been so sporadic with her jobs that I hadn't realised she was supposed to be working, or maybe I just didn't care any more about keeping up the lies. I don't know. But the moment I opened the door to the police, they covered their mouths and noses, trying to stifle their gags.

And I never saw my mother again. Either one.

58

'You came off the medication for the IVF,' Patrick says, bringing me out of my thoughts. 'We knew it was going to be a risk, but now I think that maybe it wasn't a risk worth taking.'

'What?' A hollow pit forms in my stomach.

'You're less than two weeks pregnant, with over eight months to go. Eight months of hormones disrupting your body when you've barely survived the last couple of days.'

'It's pregnancy. Everyone's hormones change. They changed during the IVF.'

'I know, I understand that, but this is different. With you, it's different. It's dangerous.'

Biles stings the back of my throat, and I have the most terrifying feeling that I already know what he's alluding to. But he can't be. He can't possibly think that, can he?

'What are you saying, Patrick? What are you trying to say to me?' Yet the way his eyes lower before he speaks confirms it all.

'I don't think going through with this pregnancy is a good idea,' he whispers.

I push myself up to standing, though I don't remember

sitting down. My legs don't seem strong enough to keep me upright, but I need to be. I need to be able to look him in the eye.

'You don't believe that. You can't.'

'Imogen, please listen.' Patrick takes my hand and lowers me back to sitting. 'I get that this is horrific, but the possibilities of what could happen are even worse. For you and the baby. I know you can see that.'

I want to respond, say I disagree, but the words are lodged in my throat. He places his hands on the side of my face, so all I can do is look at him.

'Imogen, I love you, and I can't imagine how scary this must be for you. It's so fucking cruel that you have to go through this. I'm so sorry that I ever suggested IVF. And I'm sorry because I said I'd be all right with whatever happened, but I can't. I mean... you hurt Prim, and you have no memory of it. Who's to say you wouldn't hurt yourself too? Or... or the baby?'

His words feel like daggers in my chest.

'I would never... I *could* never...' I start, but the words falter. All I can offer is empty promises. We both know that. How can I say what I am or am not capable of? Seventeen-year-old me would never have believed I could live with a dead body in the house for five days. Or conjured a vision of my mother to keep me company in my insanity. Who knows what I'm capable of now?

'It's not all in my head, Patrick. The fire at the studio, the padlock – Maureen was there.'

'I know. I know she was, but... there are other things, too. Like the *bike*,' Patrick says, his voice low.

'What are you talking about?' My head's shaking again. My thoughts rattle around in it, unable to form any cohesive order.

'You mean the pins? You think I did that? You think I gave myself a flat tyre?'

'There was no flat tyre,' he says. 'I went to replace it for you last night, but it was completely fine.'

'What?' I blink, wanting to have misheard him, but knowing I haven't. 'What do you mean, it was fine?'

'There were no pins in it. No flatness. Nothing wrong at all. Go see for yourself if you want.'

I could get up and see. I know I should, but my legs have lost the ability to move.

'No, that's not right,' I say, my mind racing. 'Someone must've replaced it. They must've.'

'When? You've been here the entire time. Unless you're saying *Maureen* did it, but I can't imagine her doing that. And you would have seen her. Heard her at least.'

I swallow hard, unsure of what to say. It doesn't make sense. How could the tyre be fine? I can vividly recall how my muscles ached as I struggled to push it. It took me hours to get home. What was I doing if not struggling to get it back?

I try to blink the tears away, but they're too fast. They form dark droplets on the table.

'What do I do? What am I supposed to do?' I ask, my voice barely audible.

Patrick stares down at the table, like he can't bear to look at me.

'I don't know,' he says softly. 'I don't know what we do next. We'll work out the steps together, but I need to go back and see Arabella. She's taking Prim to the hospital for an X-ray on her jaw.'

'Is it really that bad?' I ask, my voice small.

He nods. 'It is. It is that bad.' Silence sits in the space between us before he speaks again. 'Maybe when I'm there, I'll be able to speak to a doctor. Find out the best way, the easiest way for you to... handle this.'

The easiest way. He means the easiest way to get rid of our baby. But what choice do I have? I'm a risk to them. I'm a risk to everyone around me.

'Do you want to come with me?' he asks. 'I don't know how Prim would feel about you being there, though.'

I shake my head. Given how much I despise seeing Prim and Arabella under normal circumstances, I can't bear the thought of looking at them now.

'No, no, I'll stay.'

'Okay.' He squeezes my hand gently. 'I love you, and I know this feels impossible right now, but things'll be okay. I promise. Once you've been to the doctors. Once it's... it's over, things'll get better again. You'll get better.'

He stands, glancing at the door, and I know he's desperate to get going. To rush to be with his daughter and the ex-wife who was able to give him a child. Something I'll never be able to do.

'Come on,' he says, taking my hand and pulling me up to standing. 'You should head upstairs. Get some rest. Maybe if you fall asleep, I'll be back before you even wake up.'

I nod. That's sounds good. My body feels like it's doubled in weight since this morning. Now, all I want to do is lie down, close my eyes and not open them for a very long time.

59

I lie in bed, listening to his car drive away. As tears well in my eyes, my hands rest on my belly. How did this happen? How did I end up here? My entire life, I fought against my fear of turning into my mother. I did the right things: therapy, getting out of that shithole I grew up in, never settling for some arsehole man that would drop me the instant something better came along. I built a business, while focusing on myself and my mental health. What was all of that for, if I was just going to end up the same way as her?

The tears are running down the side of my face now, and pooling in my ears. Maybe I should follow her footsteps completely – bring the baby into the world, then end my own life. Maybe that's the best thing I can do. This baby doesn't deserve to grow up with a mother who's insane, and I don't know if I can live with the guilt of knowing I let everyone down. God, I let Patrick down so much it feels like my chest has been punctured by a thousand nails.

Sleep refuses to come. I lie there until the light fades and whatever creature it is starts stirring in the attic again. What the hell is it? Something nocturnal. That's all I know for sure. Maybe rats, though I don't know if they come out at night. Or mice either, for that matter. I guess there's one way to find out.

With a sudden sense of urgency, I sit up and swing my legs off the edge of the bed. Is it sensible to go climbing up into the attic when I'm all alone and have no idea what could be up there waiting for me? No, but I guess that's the advantage of knowing I'm insane; I don't have to do the sensible things any more.

The attic hatch is in the hallway. I'm not even sure what kind of ladder leads up to it, but I don't care. I need to know. I need to know that there's actually something up there, and that it's not my mind making up these noises, too. Even an entire rats' nest would be preferable to the way my mind is going over and over itself at the moment.

Not knowing what state the floor of the attic is going to be in, I head to the wardrobe to grab some shoes, but as I open the door, my gaze shifts to the window and my stomach lurches.

They are there again. The figure who has been watching me, and I have no intention of letting them get away.

60

I don't even put on my shoes. Instead, I bolt down the stairs and out onto the back lawn. The grass is damp on my feet and I wince as I trample on twigs and thorns, but I don't let it slow me down. I'm not letting them escape. Not again.

'What are you doing?' I shout across the field. 'Are *you* the one who started the fire? Did you put the flowers there? Why are you doing this to me?'

It's only when I reach the end of the garden that I see it's a man. He's a little older than Patrick – in his sixties, perhaps. Bile stings my throat. He's been watching me, and that's not even the worst of it. He's holding a camera. He has photos of me.

'You sick bastard. You'll go to prison for this, you know. My husband's a lawyer. You'll go to prison.'

Rather than running, like I would expect someone in his situation to do, he simply stands there.

'What?' He shakes his head as his forehead crinkles. 'No, no. You don't... you don't understand.' He blinks as he stammers. 'I'm just photographing the sky. The bats.'

'What?'

He turns the camera around to show me the screen. Dusky sky after dusky sky, and there, in each one, weaving across the tops of the shots, are the black silhouettes of bats.

Without asking, I scroll through the photos. He's right. There's nothing of me, nothing of the house, just the sky and trees and more and more bats.

'That's what you've been doing?' I ask, my voice shaking. 'You've been photographing bats?'

'I'm part of a preservation project. I've got a card. Let me find it for you.' He lowers his camera and reaches into his jacket, where he pulls out a laminated piece of cardboard. I don't read much, but the word 'bat' is written boldly on the front. That's enough for me to believe him. That and the hundreds of photos, obviously.

'Sorry if I scared you,' he says. 'Most people around here know what I do. I should have thought, though. What with you being new and everything.'

I feel a wave of embarrassment wash over me, and the pains in my feet that had felt so insignificant when I was running towards him are starting to throb. 'I'm sorry. I've just had a tough time lately. You know... the Springfield lads. They've made me their new target. I guess that happens when you move in somewhere. And there've been other things too. But anyway, I thought you were one of them. One of the Springfield lot.'

He furrows his brow. 'Springfield, you say?'

'Yeah, you know, the ones who were causing all the trouble last year with the fires.'

He shakes his head. 'Not around here, love. I've not heard of anything like that happening.'

I study his face for any sign of amusement, like he's winding me up, but if anything, he looks more confused that I'm feeling.

'Springfield Farm?' I insist, with frustration mounting. 'You must know it. It's big. They're one of the most powerful families around here.'

He shakes his head again. 'No, I've lived here all my life. There's no Springfield Farm around here. You must have the name wrong.'

My arms are covered in goosebumps and I don't know when I started shivering, but I'm not convinced it's purely because of the cold.

'No, no, I know that's what they're called. They set fire to someone's roses in Tarlton. They burned all their rose bushes down.'

The man shakes his head. 'There've been no fires around here. Not for a long time, anyway. I'd know.'

I pinch the bridge of my nose as the throbbing from my feet moves up to my temples. 'What about Maureen's shed? Last year, the fire at her place.'

'Maureen?' He frowns. 'The old lady with the big dog? She just moved in a couple of weeks ago. I'd been wondering what her name was. Kept meaning to introduce myself, but life runs away from you.'

I know he's talking, but I can barely hear. My heart is pounding that hard it's close to deafening. 'No, Maureen's lived here for close to twenty years.'

'Not here, dear,' he says gently. 'She's new. Moved in about six days before you did.'

My head spins. None of this makes sense. How? What is real and what isn't real? Is this just another hallucination? It has to be, doesn't it?

'Are you all right?' he asks, placing a hand on my arm. 'Maybe you should go inside.'

I nod, but that's the only movement I can make. If I'm not

imagining this, if I really am talking to this man with his camera and he's telling me the truth, then what does that mean? I know the answer before the question even forms in my mind. Maureen – she's the one behind all this. She must be. The fire. The flowers. She started it all. But why?

61

'My name's Leroy, by the way,' the man says as I start to walk back to the house. I didn't ask him to walk with me, but he does. Maybe he can see how unstable I look and wants to stay close in case I suddenly require catching. Maybe it's just the fastest route to his car and house. I don't ask.

'Is there a police detective living in the village?' I say instead.

'A detective?'

'Or a detective inspector, maybe? His name is Donny.'

Leroy's face creases. 'Not around here, love. The only copper we had was old Alfred over on Cherry Tree Lane. He retired, must be about twenty-five years ago. Though he still has friends in the force if you need something, but...'

'No, no, that's okay,' I say, interrupting him. 'It's fine. I'll call my husband when I get in. He shouldn't be long.'

Judging by the way his frown is still fixed in place, Leroy isn't convinced.

'You sure you're all right? You don't look well. Can I call someone for you? I got a daughter your age. I'd hate to leave her when she's not... not feeling her best.'

I could laugh. It's a sweet way of saying that I look like I've lost the plot. But I bite down on my lip, resisting the urge to show just how unsettled I am. 'No, I'm fine. I'll be fine. Thank you though. Your daughter's lucky to have a father that cares as much as you do.'

His smile is warm and though it doesn't erase the concern in his eyes, it's obvious that talking about his daughter is something Leroy loves. 'Well, I want to get a couple more snaps, so I'll be out here for another twenty minutes or so, if you change your mind.'

'Thank you, Leroy.' We've reached the edge of my garden and I can see he doesn't want to go any further, yet as he turns to leave, a thought strikes me. As far as actions go, it's weird, but I need to do it. I need to.

'Leroy, would you mind if I record everything you've just told me?' I say. 'About no Springfield farm, and when Maureen moved in. It's just... It would just help me, you see.'

I expect him to tell me to get lost or to look at me like I'm batshit crazy, but instead, the creases in his head fold back into place deeper than before.

'Are you all right, love?'

'Yes, I think so. But would you mind?'

He pauses. 'Why don't I go home, find out the dates and things – my Barb'll know all that. That way I can make sure I haven't got into a muddle. I don't want to get anyone in trouble because I've got myself mixed up, do I?'

'No, of course you don't,' I say, aware of just how awkward he looks. I'm pretty sure the only thing he's going to talk to Barb about when he gets home is the crazy woman who just accosted him while he was trying to take photos of the bats.

'Thanks, I appreciate it,' I say. 'I should get inside. My husband is probably wondering why I just raced out of the house.' I don't think Leroy is behind whatever's going on, but I'd prefer him not to know I'll be home alone tonight.

'You do that, love,' Leroy says. 'And don't worry, I'll check those dates for you.'

'Thank you.' I go to leave, but for the second time, I hesitate. 'Actually, why don't you take my telephone number? Then you can message me as soon as you find out?'

62

The minute I'm inside the house, I lock the door, then move a chair across it. I'm sure it won't be enough to stop someone who really wants to get in, but hopefully it'll be enough to give me a warning and prepare myself.

Back in the kitchen, I grab a piece of paper and a pen. I divide the page into two columns: 'Real' and 'Not Real'. But as I look at the 'Real' column, I hesitate, adding a question mark. *Am I even sure what's real any more?*

The fire – that was real. I know it was. The smoke stains on the door are proof. But the hairdryer catching fire? I was the only person who saw that, and in all my years of doing art, I've never seen anything like it. Did I imagine it? I leave that one for now.

Leroy being outside the house – that was real, too.

Prim turning up at the house – that was real. I write it down immediately, but when it comes to what happened next, I hesitate again. Did I beat up Prim? The evidence is there – her bruises – but I don't remember any of it. It's her word against mine. Reluctantly, I place it across the line, splitting it between the 'Real' and 'Not Real' columns.

I don't follow chronological order. Instead, it's just a case of which memories come to me first, and the next one is the cupboards being open. I know I went around and shut them all, but that doesn't mean I didn't open them too, did it?

Unsure where to place it, I leave that one too.

Orla has to go in the 'not real' column. There are a few different ways she could go onto the list – the visit, dumping me etc – but that would make the 'not real' column even longer and that's not something I want to do, so I just write her name once and move on. The wreath. That's the one that comes next, and it felt real. So real I can still see the flowers when I close my eyes. But did I actually pick them up? Did I feel them between my fingers? No. I didn't touch them. I just saw them, like I saw my mum helping me with homework and giving me school dinner money when she was already dead in the bath. Slowly, I write wreath in the 'not real' column, the words heavy in my chest.

Next, I think about the woman in the pharmacy, holding the very medication that I used to take. The woman who disappeared when I turned around to talk to her. As much as I don't want it to be, it's almost textbook for what happened to me before, meaning I know which column I have to write it in. Even if I don't want to.

Then there's the bike. I saw those pins. I felt the flat tyre. But now... it's fine. Patrick said it was fine. It doesn't make sense either. I put that down between the columns, too.

I've got three things fairly in the real. The rest either didn't happen or I can't be sure, and that's not including the ones like the hairdryer that I didn't write down. That doesn't feel like good odds.

But there are still more to go. The first goes in the real

column and I write it in all capitals, because I know this is true. I am pregnant. I know that is real. The test upstairs in the bathroom is confirmation of that. Not to mention Patrick was there when I took it. Unfortunately, I also know pregnancy psychosis is real too and while I don't know for certain if it's more likely in people who have experienced a psychotic break of sorts before, I have a sneaking suspicion it might be. Looking at the columns as they stand, I'd have a tough time convincing anyone I wasn't losing my mind.

So what does that mean? Do I need to give up the baby like he said? If I do, it's definitely not just a case of putting it to one side until I'm in a better place. If it is the hormones causing this, then having children is never going to happen for me. It can't.

And as for Patrick saying he would stand by me whatever, that's probably easier said than done. Our vows might have said in sickness and in health, but they didn't expect things like me beating up his daughter and not remembering it. So maybe it would be kinder if I set him free? That's what they say you should do if you love someone, isn't it? And I do. I love him with all my heart.

I go through the conversation in my head, imagining how I'm going to say it to him and how he'll respond. He's going to want to stand by me, which means I'm going to have to push him away. I can live on my own as the crazy artist – the stereotype exists for a reason. And it's better this way. I know it is.

Tears trickle down my cheeks as I imagine him putting up a protest, trying to stay, and me pushing him away. That's when my phone buzzes.

For a second, I panic, thinking it's him telling me that Prim's cheek is fractured or she needs surgery. But instead, it's an unknown number. It takes me a split second to realise who it is, though I don't really need to – the name is in the first line of the text.

> Hi, sorry, it's Leroy here. Sorry for scaring you earlier. Just wanted to let you know I checked with Barbara. Your neighbour moved in three days before you did, on the 17th, and had a group of people help her. She's kept to herself, hasn't spoken to anyone since. Also, there's no Springfield Farm anywhere near here. The nearest one is about 30 miles away. And there's no police officer other than Alfred in the villages. Lastly, the last fire Barb remembers was set by Clarence at the old vicarage in Duntisbourne, something about a chimney. No arson cases – Barb remembers everything. Hope that helps.

I stare at the message, but the words don't fully sink in. Is it because I can't believe them – or because I don't *want* to? Or perhaps it's because if I believe them, it changes everything.

I pick up my pen and write something else in the 'Real' column:

MAUREEN IS A LIAR.

Below it, I write a single question:

Why?

63

WHY? WHY? WHY?

I write the words multiple times, my scrawl getting messier and messier with every iteration.

Why would Maureen lie about these things? It doesn't make sense. But things are starting to add up, especially if I add Donny into the equation. Maureen could have timed our walk to give him enough time to get the wreath out of the house and dispose of it. I'd left the bike outside, giving anyone easy access to change the tyres and make it look like it hadn't been vandalised. Just moving those two things over to the 'Real' column makes me feel like I'm not losing my mind. But still, the question remains: *Why?* Why would Donny and Maureen want to torment me? Why would two people I've never met want to cause me so much pain? Could it be something as petty as wanting the house we bought? That seems like a ridiculous reason to go to such lengths.

I'm half-tempted to go and confront her, to demand answers. She's frail. She couldn't physically harm me. Maybe that's why she's opted for mental torture. But then there's Brutus. That dog would do whatever she asked, and I'm not about to risk that.

I can't keep this to myself. Not now that I know she is behind it. With the first spark of hope I've felt in hours, I pick up my phone, ready to ring Patrick, only to stop. If Maureen is a liar, that doesn't explain Prim's injuries. Nor does it explain why I believe I spent an entire afternoon with Orla cleaning out my studio, when she was hundreds of miles away. With everything else that's happened, it would be understandable if Patrick didn't believe me right now. But with this new information, he has to see my side of things, right?

Knowing my call won't go through, I send a text:

> Maureen is lying. She lied about the fires, about Donny, and about when she moved in. She's the one behind it. I've got evidence.

I send it and watch as the message changes to 'Delivered'. My heart pounds, waiting for it to turn to 'Read', but nothing happens. A minute ticks by and then another and it stays in that limbo of 'Delivered but not read'. Why hasn't he read it yet? I know he's got big things to deal with right now, but considering how sick he thinks I am, you'd think he'd at least want to check what I've said.

I want to switch off and distract myself with something else, but I can't. With my phone in my hand, I pace around the house for at least ten minutes when finally, after countless checks, the message changes to 'Read'.

My heart climbs up my throat. He's going to reply, right? He has to. He can't just see a message like that and ignore it, though I fear that's exactly what he's going to do when the phone starts ringing and his name flashes up on the screen.

'Imogen,' he says as soon as I answer. 'Are you okay?'

'Did you see my message? I've got evidence – evidence that Maureen is lying.'

'Lying about what?'

'Lying about *everything*. I spoke to Leroy.'

'Leroy?' Patrick's tone is one of confusion. Understandably.

'The man outside. The one I saw the other night. I didn't imagine that, Patrick. He was there, taking photos of the house. All the noise in the attic? It was bats. I went out and spoke to him, and he told me Maureen only moved in a couple of days before us. She hasn't lived here for twenty years like she said. And there haven't been any fires! She made it all up, Patrick. I don't know why, but she's the one behind all this.'

There's a pause. I can almost hear the gears turning in his mind.

'You've got evidence?' he asks.

'Yes, yes. I've got proof that she's lying – at least about the big things.'

'Okay...' he says slowly.

I'm half expecting him to apologise, to say sorry for not believing me. After all, he's my husband. He *should* believe me. But as the silence stretches out, tension replaces the space where noise should be.

'Right. Well, you need to listen to me, okay? You are *not* to go and see her. Wait until I get there. We'll go together in the morning.'

'As soon as you get here, though, right? She's not going to stop until we figure out why she's doing this. She needs to know we're on to her.'

He pauses again before he speaks. 'Okay, yes. You're right. Just don't do anything until I'm there. Stay where you are in the house and don't let on to her that you know. Okay? Promise?'

'Okay, I promise. Patrick, I love you,' I say, needing him to hear it.

'Love you too,' he replies, though I can hear the strain in his voice.

'Wait,' I add quickly before he can hang up. 'How's Prim?'

'I've not seen her. She won't speak to me. Just stay where you are, all right? We'll sort this out. We'll fix it together.'

I nod as he hangs up the phone. I get why he's still nervous. After all, there are still a lot of things I can't explain, but even though I can't figure out why yet, I know Maureen is behind it all and when I understand why, everything else will fall into place. I'm sure of it.

64

I wish I'd insisted that Patrick came straight back, but that's me being selfish. Arabella is sick. Besides, it's not like Maureen's going anywhere. She's no idea we're on to her. Still, it's hard to fall asleep, even knowing what the sound in the attic is. My adrenaline is too high.

Finally, I drift off, though I'm up before dawn, listening for the sound of Patrick's car pulling into the gravel driveway, but there's nothing. Just silence.

I check the message from Leroy is still there, then send a copy to my computer too. I'm not sure why I need it in both places. Maybe to remind myself that it really happened. To reassure myself that it's real, not just a figment of my imagination. Maureen *is* a liar, and I'm certain she's working with this Donny person. But why?

My original suspicion had been Orla, and my reasons for suspecting her were solid – she has the most to gain by pushing me back towards that darker style of painting, and nothing would have created more darkness than making me believe I would have to give up any chance of having children. And she could have lied to Patrick when she rang him too. Yes... yes, she could have told him that she was in Edinburgh and he'd have believed her. That would make sense. But how is she linked to Maureen? She lives in London, miles away. But then Maureen only moved here a few days ago, so it's conceivable that she lived in London too. There are a hundred different ways she and Orla could be connected.

I sit down at my computer, searching for any links between Orla and Maureen. Or maybe even her and Donny – not that I believe that's his real name. But nothing pops up that surprises me. Most of Orla's 'friends' aren't friends at all – they're clients, agents, people she can use to climb further up the career ladder. Thinking about it that way stings. I've never had many friends, so losing one hits hard.

After half an hour of scrolling through her social media, I find nothing and just as I'm about to give up, I hear a sing-song voice calling the name Brutus outside the door. My whole body tenses with anger.

I don't know what game Maureen has been playing, but because of her, I almost threw away my chance at having a family. I almost tossed aside Patrick, the only man I've ever loved, all because of her.

For a split second, I consider waiting for Patrick, but as I turn my head, I glance at the kitchen worktop and my eyes fall on the knife block. One thing is for certain: I've been underestimating Maureen.

I stand up and move over to the counter, where I pick up one of the knives and slip it into my bag. I won't be underestimating her again.

65

I don't feel scared as I walk out into the field with the knife in my bag. I'm not sure what I plan on doing with it. Defend myself, I guess, if Brutus comes for me. I've never imagined myself hurting an animal before, and I sure as hell hope it doesn't happen now, but I'm not taking risks. Not when it comes to Maureen. If there's anything I've learned about my neighbour, it's that I've seriously underestimated her.

'Imogen.' Her smile broadens when she sees me walking over to her. 'I was just going to go in and put the kettle on. Fancy a cuppa?'

'I know it's you, Maureen. Why? Why are you doing it?'

She tilts her head to the side, looking remarkably like an owl. 'Sorry, love, I'm not sure what you're on about.'

I scoff. Even now, she's still trying to play me for a fool.

'I had a conversation with Leroy last night. You'll know him, won't you? He works with the bat conservation and takes lots of photos of them. He's lived in the village since he was a lad. You must know him.'

She rolls her eyes. 'Bats, is that what he's telling you he's doing this week? God, the man's batty, but that's about the only truth in there. Got a screw loose, that one. Last year, he was documenting all the planes. He thought we were being spied on. The time before that, he kept saying he'd spotted a black panther. Even left meat out for the bloody things too. Whole circuses, right on the roadside. Never married, poor man, but I guess that's what happens when you live on your own. Even been a widower a long time, that one.'

'Stop lying to me!' I yell. She stops, her eyes widening. 'You're lying to me. Every word that's come out of your mouth has been a lie. There's no Springfield Farm near here. I looked. The nearest one is in Gloucester. It's almost thirty miles away.'

Her smile falters a little, but it doesn't disappear. Instead, she shrugs the comment off. 'Oh, well, maybe it changed its name. I don't know. It was Springfield Farm when I moved here.'

'Three days before us, you mean?' For the first time, I see a flicker in her eyes. She's doing a great job of lying, I'll give her that, but she's still lying.

'I know, Maureen. I know that you moved here just before we did. That Donny's not a policeman – I can't even believe that I thought he was. I mean, he asked me zero relevant questions. You're the one who started the fire. You're the one who ordered the wreath. Did you puncture my bike's tyres too? How much of it was you, Maureen?'

She presses her lips tightly together as she looks at me.

'Having a baby is tough, I get that. My daughter, she struggled. I mean, hers was a little more complicated, but I understand. It's probably the hormones that are doing this to you, dear. I mean, if I'd wanted to hurt you, I could have slipped something into your tea. And why would I have put the fire out if I wanted something to happen to you? You're not okay, love. You're not. It's the pregnancy, I'm sure. Let me guess, morning sickness has been so bad you haven't eaten properly for days. Lack of food will do that to you, you know. Maybe you're seeing things. And have you got the reflux yet? Oh, that was the worst of it. What we go through with our bodies... Men will never understand. And it doesn't stop with the children either. No, there's menopause and all that to come after. Come on, let's go into the house. Patrick will be here soon.'

As she moves back towards the house, I shake my head. I know what she's doing – speaking constantly, firing questions so I don't have a chance to get my thoughts straight – but I have to. I have to block out all her words. I have to focus on what I know is true. And I know there's no Springfield Farm. I looked at the map myself. Maureen lied to me and she's still lying. I just don't understand why.

'Is it Orla?' I say. 'Is she the reason you're behind this?'

'Orla? You mentioned her before, didn't you? It's good that you have people around you. You need that. I wish my daughter had had more people around her. She's got them now, though.'

That's when it clicks. Goosebumps rise on my arms.

'Your daughter? You don't have a daughter. You said you didn't have any children.'

'I did, didn't I? Strange that, because I do. And I'm finally going to be able to get her the justice she deserves.'

66

Smiles are a strange expression, aren't they? They're one of the reasons I used to enjoy painting portraits so much – because of the smiles. People always assume they are locked to the lips, maybe flickering to the eyes too, but there is so much more to them. The way cheeks draw inwards or push up can tell you so much about the true meaning behind the expression. Whether it's genuine. Whether it's polite or heartfelt. Then there are the lips, the amount of teeth on show, and the tension around the jaw. That's before you start looking at the eyes and the manner in which the skin around them does or doesn't crease. A smile can convey a thousand different emotions, and the one I'm looking at now is doing exactly that.

The left side of Maureen's mouth is slanted far higher than the right. It's more of a sneer than an actual smile, and that sliver of exposed teeth only reinforces that.

'Your daughter?' I say as a chill spreads down my spine. 'You think I did something to your daughter?'

'Oh, I don't think. I know,' she says, before turning around and striding towards her house.

'Wait, what are you doing?' I race after her and grab her by the shoulder, but the minute my palm makes contact, Brutus growls. Spittle drips down his bared teeth.

'I'd let go of me if I were you,' Maureen says. 'You won't be able to paint any of your pictures without that arm, will you?'

I glance down at Brutus. The whites of his eyes gleam as they glower at me, though the second I let go of his owner, the snarling stops.

'I'm glad you did the sensible thing,' Maureen says, flashing me a smile before she continues walking to her house. For a moment, I stand there and watch her, unsure if I should follow. She wants me to. I can tell that much. She wants me to follow her into the house, onto her own turf, and I know that's the only way I'm going to get answers. Before I move, I slip the knife from my bag to my pocket, making sure it's within reach. I might have underestimated Maureen, but she's underestimated me too, and if it comes to that, I'll prove it.

'Squashed fly biscuit?' she says as I step into her kitchen.

'No, what I want is answers,' I say.

'I can tell. You're quite insistent, aren't you?'

She moves forward and fills the kettle before switching it on. Boiling water – another weapon she can use against me, or I can use against her if needs be.

She stands there with her back to me, looking at the walls.

'Who's your daughter, Maureen?' I ask. 'Because whatever you think I've done to her, I haven't. I haven't. I don't even know who she is.'

'Oh, and that should make it better, should it?' she says, letting out a scoff. 'Maybe if you'd taken a bit of time to get to know her, you wouldn't have done what you did.'

'But I don't know what I did! Please, if you could just tell me. If you could tell me so I understand.'

As she stands there, she pulls down two mugs from the cupboard. Another potential weapon, perhaps. Throw the tea? Or smash the mug so that I have some sort of shiv to use? They're both possibilities.

'Do you think... do you think that maybe you've got it wrong?' I say. I realise it's probably not the most sensible thing to say to a crazy woman, but she's not giving me any answers and I'm at a loss for what to do. If nothing else, I need to keep her talking until Patrick gets here and he can step in. I wish I'd told him to call the police when we spoke. Or called them myself before I'd come here, but it's too late for that now. There'll be plenty of time for the police once I've got answers.

'Maureen, whatever you think I'm responsible for, I'm sure it's a mix up.'

As she turns to face me, her eyes are little more than narrow slits.

'There's no mix up. You broke her when you killed her child and then—'

'What are you on about?' I snap. Under normal circumstances, there is no chance I would just interrupt someone who is suffering from some clearly dangerous delusions, but if I can just make her see that she's very wrong here, then maybe I can get her to back down before.

'I don't know what you're on about. I promise – I've never killed anybody. Not a child. Not an adult. Nobody.' I know there was that blip when my mother died, but other than that, I've been in full control of my faculties for my entire life. Killing someone is not something I would have forgotten. She's crazy. That's the only explanation. She's been terrorising me because of some delusion that I somehow harmed her daughter.

'Maureen, I'm sorry.' My tone is gentle for the first time since I came here demanding answers. Sure, she's crazy and tried to ruin my life, but she's obviously been through stuff. 'Whatever you and your daughter went through, it sounds terrible, but you've got the wrong person.'

A cold, sharp laugh croaks from Maureen's throat and resounds through my bones.

'Really? Now is the time you're telling me this?' she sneers. 'If I'm wrong, then why don't you tell me who – twenty-two years ago – called the authorities and had a darling little grandchild taken away?'

As her eyes lock on mine, I feel all the heat drain from my body. She's right. I am the one she's after.

67

'I don't understand,' I whisper. My voice shakes as I force the words up and out of my throat, which is now bone dry. 'I... I was helping.'

'Helping?' Maureen laughs – a high-pitched, nasal rasp that scrapes through my ears like nails on a chalkboard. 'They took her away. She's dead because of you.'

'No. No. The mother – she was abandoning the child. Leaving them all night to cry by herself.'

'A couple of hours!' Maureen shouts at me. 'She left her for a couple of hours at most. She needed some space. A little bit of air, that's all. You have no idea how difficult it is to raise a child.'

I try to swallow, but my body won't respond to anything I ask of it. All I can manage is a stutter of protest. 'No, but... but...'

'But what?' Maureen spits. 'You didn't ask. Just like they didn't bother to ask. No. They took the child away from her, like they knew best, but they didn't know about her allergies. They didn't know that milk made her sick. They took that tiny baby away from my daughter and gave her a bottle of normal formula, then left her thinking she would just go to sleep. That poor little baby never woke up again.'

It feels like the contents of my stomach have curdled. As if my very core is turning more and more rotten with every rancid breath.

'Maureen… I couldn't have known. I was – I was ten years old. I—'

'That's no excuse!' she shrieks. 'You swan around life painting your pretty little pictures, oblivious to what the rest of us go through. My poor little Ella. And then, as if that wasn't bad enough, you destroyed her life all over again.'

'What—'

My head spins. My vision blurs.

'What are you talking about?'

I wait for her to answer, but before she does, there's a hammering at the door.

'Maureen, it's Patrick. Let me in.'

My heart clenches in my chest as I fear she might say no. After all, in her head, I'm responsible for killing her granddaughter. But she doesn't. Instead, she smiles broadly.

'Well, that's perfect timing, wouldn't you say?' she asks, before moving to the front door.

While her back is turned to me, I check for the knife again. I know it can't have gone, and I still don't know how I plan on using it, but I need to feel it there.

The second the door clicks open, Patrick pushes Maureen to the side and races towards me.

'Thank God you're all right,' he says. I collapse into his arms. A sob that I had kept tight within me surfaces. Yet before I can say anything, he has let go of me and is facing Maureen.

'What the hell were you doing, Mo?' he demands, his face like thunder.

Considering Patrick is a fuming, fully grown man, I expect the little woman to look somewhat fearful, or at the very least intimidated. But she doesn't. Instead, she just looks at him with a sense of utter calm.

'I told her, Patrick,' she says, an insane smile glinting in her eyes.

'Mo...' he says, for a second time. I've never heard him call her that before, and it makes my skin inexplicably prickle. Yet it's Maureen's absolute ease that makes me even more nervous.

'I told her,' she says again, nodding as she speaks. 'I told her what she did to Arabella's child.'

68

Patrick is staring at me, while Maureen reaches down and strokes Brutus. I'm frozen to the spot, trying to make sense of what she's just said to me.

Arabella's child? Surely she's mistaken. She must be talking about a different Arabella, surely? That's the only thing I can think of.

I switch my gaze from Patrick to Maureen and back again, unsure where to settle my sight. Any second now, I'm sure that Patrick is going to tell her she's crazy. That she needs help, the way I know she does. But he doesn't. Instead, his lips part slightly, as if he's struggling to force any words out. When one finally does, it's enough to make my heart crack in two.

'I'm sorry, Imogen,' he whispers.

It feels like all the air has been drawn from the room. My lungs are struggling to pull in a single breath. My chest is so tight it's as if it's been bound. And my mind. There are so many questions filling my head, but one thought is circling over and over and over again.

Finally, my throat chokes it out.

'You knew she was doing this to me?' I say, inching away from him and towards the window. 'You knew she was doing this to me... You... You...'

'Imogen, please—' He steps forward, trying to grab my hands, but I flick him away.

'You were doing this, too. You were in on it.'

'No! No!' he says, shaking his head frantically. 'Please. You need to listen to me. You need to understand.'

My legs and hands are trembling so much that I have to brace my weight against the door just to stay upright. Even when I knew what Maureen had done, and why, there had still been hope. Because Patrick was coming. He was coming home. And he was going to make sure I was safe. Now I see I couldn't have been more wrong. I move to leave, but Patrick grabs my arm.

'Please, Imogen. I need you to listen to me. I promise – I didn't know. It was only when I came here and saw Maureen that first day. And I've been trying to stop her. I have.'

He's looking at me like he expects me to reply, but I don't know how. My breath catches and croaks.

'Everything... Everything has been a lie,' I say finally.

'Not everything,' Patrick says quickly. 'Please, I promise you, not everything.'

Maureen stands at the back of the room, that same slanted sneer still twisting her face.

'It hurts, doesn't it?' she says. 'Hurts discovering how much power a single person can have to destroy your whole life.'

'Mo, shut it,' Patrick snaps before he turns back to me. 'Imogen, I love you. And I'm sorry I didn't tell you about Arabella, about the baby. But I didn't see what good it would do, you know. This doesn't change anything between us. Nothing at all.'

'Of course it does!' He's got to be screwing with me, right? There's no way he could possibly think I'd ever let myself be alone with him again. He let her terrorise me. He let me think I was going insane. Who the hell does that, let alone to someone they are having a child with?

'Please, just come home with me,' he begs. 'We can talk through it. It will all make sense.'

'I'm not going anywhere with you,' I say.

He flinches, as if my words actually hurt him. As if there was anything I could say that would hurt him after what he'd done to me.

'Can we just... sit down?' he asks. 'Talk about it?'

'I'm leaving,' I say. 'I'm leaving and I'm going to the police. About both of you. About your whole fucking family.'

I turn towards the door, but before I can move, Maureen steps into my path, blocking the way. Brutus is at her side. I get the feeling that one wrong word from me and she'll set him on me. I suspect half of her is actually hoping for that.

'You're not going anywhere,' she says.

Patrick grabs me by the shoulder and pulls me to the side so that he is standing square on to Maureen.

'Mo, that's enough. She knows. She knows what she did. You've scared her shitless. That's enough.'

'Enough?' She laughs. 'Oh, I'm not nearly done. Do you have any idea how long I've waited for this?' Her eyes glower, though this time her venom is directed at him, not me. 'You were meant to help us,' she hissed. 'If you'd just done what you were supposed to do, we'd never be here.' She shifts her gaze back to me. 'I think we should sit down. Sit down so that you can hear how the man you love only came into your life to deceive you. And then, at the end of it, I'll decide which, if either of you, I'm going to let live.'

Then she slips her hand onto the window ledge and pulls out the gun.

69

'Patrick?' I say, barely able to force out his name. I don't know what I'm even saying it for. To help me? No, I don't want that man to help me with anything ever again, but then I don't want to die either and right now I know there's a better chance of us getting out alive if we work together. And yet he now seems to be the one who is frozen to the spot, unable to move.

'Come on, you two,' Maureen says, her voice scarily chirpy. 'Let's have a seat. Then you can tell Imogen here about your part in all this. How it was never a coincidence that you came to her exhibitions. How it was never a coincidence that you ended up in bed with her?'

'Stop it!' he yells, but as his eyes meet mine, I can see it. The guilt. The shame. The truth of Maureen's words.

'It started that way,' he admits, his voice low and trembling.

'Not yet. Let's sit down first.' Maureen waggles the gun in front of us and this time, I move. It was one thing thinking I could stand a chance against her and Brutus with my kitchen knife with Patrick on my side. Now I've seen she's got a gun, I'm not sure even the pair of us would be able to do anything.

Upon Maureen's orders, Patrick takes a seat next to me, and I watch as his hand flickers out towards me, only for him to change his mind. Instead, he exhales shakily.

'Tell her,' Maureen says. 'Tell her everything.'

His Adam's apple bobs up and down as his chin nods. The slight jerk causes a stray tear to escape and roll down his cheeks, but I don't feel the slightest hint of pity for him. I can't. I don't think I even know the man sitting in front of me.

'I met Arabella just after her baby was taken,' he starts. 'It was meant to be a casual thing. And it was. But then she got pregnant with Prim. I wasn't keen on becoming a dad, but she told me what happened to the other baby, and I—' He swallows hard. 'I did the right thing. I did the right thing by staying with her.' He pauses to sniff and wipe his tears, and I think that maybe he's waiting for me to say something, too. When I don't, he carries on. 'We had some good times,' he says. 'Really good times, but it was all sporadic. Every time I thought things had settled down, when I thought I knew how to make her happy, she would flick again. Sink inside herself and get lost in the past. I get it. She was traumatised. She needed proper help, but she refused to get any. That's why I sent Prim to boarding school. Because she was getting to an age where she would see things, understand things, and I didn't want that for her.' His head jerks upwards and he looks at Maureen, a strange expression crossing his face.

'Prim,' he says. 'Imogen didn't do anything to Prim, did she?'

Maureen's chuckle is dry and venomous.

'Oh no, my darling Primrose. Such a lovely girl. So lucky to have a grandmother like me.' She smirked at me. 'I told Arabella I'd wanted to let her in on what I was up to, ever since I approached the farmer about renting this cottage. But Arabella wanted to protect her child. Like any good mother would.

Because she is a wonderful mother, even though you took that chance away from her once.' My eyes flicker down to look at the gun in her hand. She's holding it casually across her knee, like it doesn't have the power to kill everyone in this room. Her nonchalance is almost as terrifying as the gun. Still, I try not to hide my fear as she carries on. 'I would have kept my word to Arabella and left Prim out of it, but then she turned up the other day when Donny was here. Her Uncle Donny, and he spilled the beans.'

'Donny is your son?' I said.

Her grin is insane. 'He's ex-police. Very good boy. That's how he had the contacts to get me this.'

She taps her gun against her thigh, and this time I can't help but flinch.

'And it was very handy to have Prim to talk to about things. Like when I told her you suspected your friend Orla. We figured we could use that, which was why I got her to ring you,' she says, looking at Patrick. 'From what I hear our Prim did a wonderful job pretending to be an art agent, or whatever it is she does.'

'That was Prim?' Patrick rubs his forehead as he speaks, like he's trying to make her words sink in and make sense to him. 'You made me think Imogen was really going crazy. That she had really got sick again.'

'And you made her think that you genuinely liked her art.'

A guttural sound escapes his throat as his entire body trembles. I've never heard him sound so angry before.

'I told Imogen she should end the pregnancy,' he cries. 'And you got my daughter involved in all of this. I always thought you were a little on the crazy side, but you're not at all, are you? You're evil.'

Maureen scoffs and rolls her eyes like Patrick is completely exaggerating what's going on here.

'Anyway, we're not talking about Prim and Donny, are we, Patrick? We're talking about you. How you seduced a young woman with the intention of ruining her... only to bottle it. Like the coward you are. After all, if you'd had any balls you would have told Imogen here who I was straight away, wouldn't you? But no, you didn't, because you were scared of what she'd do when she found out. I bet you're wishing you'd told her now, though, aren't you?'

Patrick doesn't respond to her. Instead, he's looking at me.

'I'm sorry. I'm so sorry, Im,' he says. Tears now tumble freely down his cheeks, but it's only when I look down and see the dark circles on my jeans that I realise he's not the only one who's crying. Hastily, I try to wipe away the evidence of my emotion.

'Is Arabella even sick?' I say, directing my question to the pair. Patrick goes to reply, only to stop and look at his ex-mother-in-law. Maureen's left eyebrow arches.

'I may have suggested to Arabella that you spin that little web to keep you away from the house. You know, so I could get to know Imogen a little more.'

From the way Patrick's head drops, I can tell he didn't know. He really believed Arabella was sick, and they pulled the wool over his eyes. Well, more fool him. He should have known better, considering he was in the middle of the vipers' pit when all this started.

'If you wanted to kill me, why haven't you done it already?' I say, glancing at the gun. 'You could have let the fire burn me. Ended it all then. Why all this?'

Maureen nods and scratches at her head, as if she's considering the question.

'I did think about it,' she says. 'I was very close actually, listening to you screaming, knowing you were trapped with no way out. But that had never been the plan. I needed to break you first. I needed you to understand the consequence your actions had had. It's not about the death, you see. It's not just about how you murdered my granddaughter. It's about how you broke my darling Arabella. And making him pay, too.'

She glances at Patrick, and there's nothing but pure venom in her eyes. 'She trusted you. We all did. And you betrayed that trust. Now it's time to reap what you sow. For both of you.'

That's the moment I see it. Her hand tightens her grip on the gun. The muscles in her shoulder tense as if she's about to lift her arm. My mouth opens, ready to let out a scream, yet before I can, Patrick is diving across the room, straight towards Maureen. A heartbeat later, I hear the gun fire.

70

For a split second, time slows so much it feels like it has almost stopped entirely.

As Patrick lunges forward, his back blocks the view of the gun so that all I can see is Maureen's virulent snarl that tightens further as the shot runs out. Then, in that slowed space of time, I watch as a small circle of red spreads out on Patrick's back.

I bought that shirt, I think. I bought that shirt and now it's ruined. I don't know why that's the thought that hits me first, but it doesn't last for long as in the same instant, Patrick's body slumps down, landing directly on Maureen.

As she lets out a wail, Brutus jumps forward in an attempt to help his owner. I move to do the same. Not to help Maureen, but ready to lift Patrick off her and see if there is a way to save him, but before I so much as touch his shoulder, I stop.

Almost the entire back of the shirt is now soaked with blood. Even if I didn't move him, even if he, by some miracle, is still breathing, there is no way I can keep him alive until the ambulance arrives, and even if I could, right now, Patrick is not my priority. I am.

The old woman is pinned in place, her arm trapped beneath Patrick's body. She heaves, trying to push him off, and another shot fires out. I don't know where it goes, but it doesn't get me, and that's what I care about. She can't shoot me like this. Trapped beneath Patrick. She can't hurt me like this.

'You killed him,' I say quietly, the reality of what I have just seen sinking in.

'I will kill you too. Mark my words,' Maureen spits. 'Brutus, do you hear me? She needs to pay. She needs to pay!'

The dog isn't listening. He's focused only on getting his owner the help he thinks she needs, pushing at Patrick, trying to roll the man off her. But even with all his animal strength, the angle is too difficult.

I realise this is my only chance. I draw the knife from my pocket, and for a moment, I consider plunging it into the animal. But I change my mind. Brutus isn't going to leave her. Killing him would do nothing except put me closer to Maureen, and that's the last thing I want. I need to save myself. I need to get out of here.

Before I can move, though, another thought flashes through my mind. I could take the knife to Maureen's throat and make sure she can never hurt me or anyone I care about again. I can show her and the rest of her screwed-up family what happens if you come after me. I can end this. That's what I think. Only once again, I change my mind. Despite what she might believe, I am not a murderer. And I won't let her make me one. Instead, I bolt for the front door and slam it behind me.

'We're going to be okay. We're going to be okay,' I say, unsure if I'm talking to the baby or myself. Probably both. Either way, the words help drown out the hammering of my heart.

I've just reached Maureen's gate when I hear a heavy thud from inside the house. My heart lurches. If that's what I think it is – if she's just got Patrick off her – then she's going to be coming after me. And it doesn't matter how fast I am compared to the old woman. It's how fast I am compared to the bullets in her gun that matter. Meaning I need to get out of here.

With every inch of strength I have left, I race towards my car, keys in hand, beeping the fob repeatedly so I know the doors are unlocked. I jump inside and pull the door closed, only for a bang to reverberate through the car, so loud it makes my ears ring.

I gasp at the noise, though for a split second, I think it's just the sound of me slamming the door – until I see the rear windscreen has shattered. Maureen is standing there. Gun in hand. Immediately, there's another shot. This one accompanied by the ting of metal, telling me she hit somewhere else on the car. She's not going to stop firing. And all it takes is one of those bullets to end mine and my baby's life.

Without giving myself the chance to second-guess it, I put my foot on the clutch, shift into reverse, and slam down on the gas.

I watch her in the rearview mirror the entire time. Watch as her image grows larger and larger. She's so focused on me, so focused on shooting at me, that she doesn't even realise I'm coming for her. Not until I'm just metres away. Only then do I see the horror flash on her face.

She dives to the side, but I yank the steering wheel and the back of the car swings round to collide with her shoulder. A loud scream bellows out into the night. A scream that tells me she's still alive, and if she's alive, she can still come for me and my unborn child. I move the car forward a few feet, just enough to see where she is. Then I reverse again at the exact angle I need for the wheels to make full contact with her prone body.

This isn't murder. It's self-defence.

71

Only once I'm sure that Maureen isn't going to get up and try firing at me again, do my legs finally find the momentum to leave. I drive my car out of the lane. My plan was to drive into town, find the police station, and actually speak to someone there. But my body is shaking so much that I struggle to keep the wheels on the road. The last thing I want, after everything I've been through, is to end up crashing the car.

When I get to the village, I park up on the green and knock on the nearest door.

'I need you to take me to Leroy,' I say the second it opens.

'Are you all right, love?' the woman asks. I don't know what the time is, but she's already got a dressing gown on and looks more than a little confused by me standing on her doorstep. But I don't have time for people to be confused.

'Leroy!' I shout this time. 'Do you know where he is?' I turn around on the spot, shouting out towards the village green. 'Leroy! Leroy!'

In a place this small, I'm sure that someone will hear, and

yet before any of the other doors open, the woman is ushering me to a small cottage almost opposite hers.

'He's just over here. Come on. I'm taking you there now.'

Minutes later I'm walking into another cottage.

'Just sit down,' Leroy's wife, Barbara, says, leading me over to an armchair. 'I'll get you a drink, don't worry.'

'Alfred and some of the lads have gone up to the house,' Leroy says when he joins us a few minutes later. He had disappeared as soon as I'd finished telling him about Patrick and Maureen. Or at least, telling him as much as I could in my stuttering, barely coherent manner. *Dead. Gun.* I know I got those words out several times. Along with *dangerous* and *liar*. Beyond that, I can't be sure what I said.

The fearful part of me worried he had gone to the house and been Maureen's next victim, so seeing him here caused a brief flutter of relief within me.

'They're going to make sure it's all secure for the police when they get here,' he continues. 'I can go too, or I can stay here with you. Whatever you want.'

'I... I...'

'You shush,' Barbara says gently. Unlike her husband, she seems to understand that I am in no position to make any decisions. 'It'll be all right. Just wait and see.'

It isn't long before I hear the sirens wailing in the distance, knowing they are heading to the place that, for a few days, I had called home. Knowing they are going to find my husband, dead from a gunshot wound, and an old woman with the murder weapon in her hand, and her bones broken as she lays crushed to death on her driveway.

They'll find Brutus, too, I think. While the rest of my mind refuses to focus on anything that has happened to me, I can't help but wonder what will happen to the animal now, after loving her so dearly.

When I think of the three of them at that cottage – Patrick, Maureen, and Brutus – it is Brutus I felt the sorriest for.

He hadn't known what kind of family he was coming into. Just like he won't understand why he is now without the person he loved. And in some strange way, I know exactly how he feels.

EPILOGUE

'Glass of champagne, madam?' the waitress asks, before her cheeks colour red as she notices my bump. 'Sorry, orange juice?'

'No, thank you.' But she doesn't leave immediately. Instead, she lingers and surveys the scene. The paintings hung on the white walls. The men and women dressed in their finery as they amble around, sipping their drinks and taking in one work of art and then another.

'They're beautiful, aren't they,' she says. 'You know, I read an article about the paintings. Well, about the artist. Her husband's previous family tried to kill her for something she did when she was a child. It was really dark, actually.'

'Is that right?' I avoid her eyes as I speak.

'Yeah, it's incredible, don't you think? I mean, I look at these paintings, and there's so much light in them. You wouldn't think that someone who had gone through all that would still have that kind of light, would you?'

I look at one of the pictures. One of my favourites. Most of the canvas is grey, but there in the corner are the brightest streaks of light, like the sun, breaking through the clouds. Even though those brushstrokes take up a minute area of the entire work, it's all I can focus on. It's all anyone can focus on.

'I guess light is where you look for it,' I said, resting my hands on my stomach. A moment later, she moves on.

'Twenty minutes.'

I turn to the side to see Orla standing beside me.

'Sorry?' I say.

'Twenty minutes. That's how long it took you to sell out. I guess I was wrong. All your paintings have a market.'

It's not quite that straightforward, and both she and I know it.

'Let's be honest,' I say. 'These have a market because of the magazine article.'

Orla smiles. 'Maybe the article played a little part, but they still would have sold out, anyway.'

For a moment, she stays there, standing and staring at the painting.

'So, you're all moved back okay?'

'Yup, everything is in place. I thought maybe you could come over for a couple of drinks later in the week. Soft ones, anyway. I don't know when I'll have much of a chance to socialise after this one arrives. And actually... actually, I'm thinking about moving. Hopefully, before she comes.'

'Again? You've just got your old flat back.'

'I know, and I'll keep it for when I'm in London. But I fancy trying something different. Like the south of France.'

As Orla raises her eyebrows, a flutter of fear flickers within me. These last six months have been a blur. Patrick is gone. Arabella and Prim got suspended sentences, and there are restraining orders on them that I will keep in place forever.

'Is that a good idea?' she says.

I shrug. I think so.

Mentally, I am fine. Okay, fine is a bit too much. Everything I went through has definitely taken its toll and there's a bit of paranoia, but the shrink says that's to be expected. And I'm seeing her twice a week, three times when things get tough. She's the one who suggested Orla and I reconnect, and also recommended I do the article.

'Well then,' she says. 'South of France it is. And I promise you, I will help you set up your studio this time too. And we can even take a photo, so that you have the evidence of it there.'

I let out a slight laugh. It's good. To be able to talk about it like this. To make light of things. I'm pretty sure it's the only way I'm going to be able to move forward, and this baby is going to be the reason I never look back again.

* * *

ACKNOWLEDGEMENTS

As always, my most heartfelt thanks go to you, my readers. I am so grateful for every journey you come along with me, and your support is so deeply appreciated. Thank you.

Thank you to Emily, my wonderful editor, and the team at Boldwood Books.

And lastly to my incredible family and friends who constantly support and uplift me. I am so lucky to have each and every one of you in my life.

ABOUT THE AUTHOR

H. M. Lynn writes tense, gripping psychological thrillers with her signature engaging and emotionally rich storytelling. She also writes in many other genres including romance, as Hannah Lynn.

Sign up to H. M. Lynn's mailing list for news, competitions and updates on future books.

Visit H. M. Lynn's website: www.hannahlynnauthor.com

Follow H. M. Lynn on social media:

facebook.com/hannahlynnauthor
instagram.com/hannahlynnwrites
bookbub.com/authors/hannah-lynn

Printed in Dunstable, United Kingdom

63372923R00157